"FASCINATING"
Chicago Tribune

"To your good health, Doctor," said Lieutenant MacMann, raising his glass to me.

"That's an appropriate toast," I said. "I'm beginning to think my health is in jeopardy."

I picked up the handkerchief and unwrapped the dart, handing it to him. He took it carefully in both hands, stared down at it under the lamp, then looked up to meet my eyes.

"It's curare. I'm sure."

I stared at Lieutenant MacMann, wondering whether twelve-year-old Stelgis was as innocent as I imagined—or the most dangerous psychopath I had ever known.

THE ADAM SLEEP

WINFRED VAN ATTA

AVON
PUBLISHERS OF BARD, CAMELOT AND DISCUS BOOKS

All of the characters in this book are fictitious, and any resemblance to actual persons living or dead, is purely coincidental.

AVON BOOKS
A division of
The Hearst Corporation
959 Eighth Avenue
New York, New York 10019

Copyright © 1980 by Winfred Van Atta
Published by arrangement with Doubleday & Company, Inc.
Library of Congress Catalog Card Number: 79-7781
ISBN: 0-380-53744-3

First Avon Printing, March, 1981

AVON TRADEMARK REG. U.S. PAT. OFF. AND IN
OTHER COUNTRIES, MARCA REGISTRADA, HECHO EN
U.S.A.

Printed in the U.S.A.

Dedicated to:

Jimmy Eaton and his parents, who touched my life gently, felt the warts and remained my dear friends throughout the years.

When does night end
And day begin
Where does the Amazon
Become the Sea
How long did Adam Sleep
Waiting for Eve?
—*Dr. James Scott*
(from *The Making of Mankind*)

Chapter One

Among the unlisted privileges extended to residents in psychiatry at the University of Manhattan Medical Center is the frequent opportunity to work an extra eight to ten hours on what is euphemistically called their day off. Such privileges usually come in the form of a godfather offer from Dr. Leon Karsloff, professor and chairman of the department and director of the Psychiatric Institute. It is never an offer to be taken lightly, especially by a second-year resident who has not been conspicuous in volunteer programs and who has often been accused of undue attention to the social needs of off-duty nurses at Hadley Hall. . . . All of which is a circuitous way of explaining why I found myself crossing George Washington Bridge at 5 A.M. on a Monday in early July, en route to Hanover State Hospital in the Catskill Mountains.

I was still feeling twinges of anger as I headed up Palisades Interstate Parkway and remembered Dr. Karsloff's instructions, given in that intimidating voice he uses when he's displeased. And he wasn't exactly jumping with joy to get my call at 4 A.M. at his home in Leonia, New Jersey. He had been trying to reach me since late Sunday afternoon and had finally come to Butler Tower to leave the keys of his car with my friend Yong Ha, alone with instructions to call him at whatever hour I arrived.

When I came through the revolving door at 3:45 A.M.,

Yong Ha was waiting for me. His eyes were condemning me, and his clip-on bow tie jumped rhythmically over his agitated Adam's apple as he worked himself up to another verbal explosion. I raised a hand to restrain him, but past training and conditioning were forgotten.

"Okay, Glom," he cried, putting the 'l' of my last name in the wrong place as usual. "That somnoblitch, go to hell in basket, Karsloff! That mother—"

"Stop it right there! No more 'mother' words. Can't you remember anything we talked about? Now let me have it. Gently, though."

He wilted, looking sheepishly down at the toes of his brightly polished shoes, wet his lips again and said, "You call Karsloff quick. Telephone four times, madder than by god."

I took the car keys and telephone slip and retreated backward into the elevator, then pushed the fourteenth-floor button.

Yong Ha is a student at the medical center's School of X-Ray Technology, from which he will graduate in a few months and return to his adoptive parents in Hawaii. He works the tower desk, for which he receives his apartment, a weekly stipend and his meals at the student's cafeteria. He took me under his wing after I offered to help him with his speech problem. He disapproves of my life-style, often forgetting to relay messages left by those people of whom he disapproves. He lives only two doors from my two-room corner apartment, in which he sometimes cooks us exotic oriental dinners. He checks lecture and seminar schedules, often awakening me in time to attend them, even though I usually need sleep far more than medical indoctrination. Yong had learned his basic English from an infantry company stationed in his native Korea. As one of the countless war orphans there, he had been taken in as the company's mascot when he was five. When the company returned to its base in Hawaii, its top sergeant had legally adopted him. The sergeant had married a Chinese girl, who had taught Yong cooking skills, but she had not been able to overcome his speech problem. Most of the time he speaks broken English, but when angry or excited, he reverts to U.S. Army English, punctuating each statement with an obscenity. I worry almost as much about him and his future as I do mine. If he's going to succeed, he's got to learn to control his speech.

I was still thinking of Yong Ha as I entered my apartment, wondering if I dare ignore Dr. Karsloff's message and blame it on Yong for failing to relay it. I decided against it, though, even though I know Yong would accept blame for carelessness to protect me. I wanted only to flop on my bed and lose my multiple problems in sleep; instead, I went to the bathroom to wash my face in cold water. Finally, I want to my phone and dialed the New Jersey number. When Dr. Karsloff answered on the first ring, I knew that it wouldn't be a pleasant conversation.

"Just where in the name of God have you been, Golm? I've been lying here wide awake for five solid hours waiting for your call."

"I had duty at the emergency room yesterday," I said. "I was just leaving when they brought in this battered child. His mother put his little fingers in the gas flame to teach him not to play with the stove when she's downstairs working go-go at El Centro Bar on—"

"Don't tell me what I already know! I've been trying to contact you since early last evening. That Chinese clerk at the tower said—"

"He's Korean, sir, not—"

"Shut up, goddamnit and listen! He said he thought you were at the library researching your paper."

"Do you have any reason to doubt him, sir?"

"You're damned right I do! At a quarter of seven you and Miss Margaret Bochmeir were observed carrying a blanket and a picnic basket from Hadley Hall to her Cadillac. The desk clerk said you were going to Bear Mountain Park. You still weren't back at midnight. Falstein tells me you are out four nights a week and that you're no stranger among the student nurses and our LPN's. Have you thought of willing your body to the Institute for the Study of Human Reproduction? Think about it seriously."

"I—I'm sorry I wasn't back early, sir. I never dreamed anyone would want to contact me. I have today off and—"

"You can forget that right now. I want you to take my car and drive up to Hanover State Hospital to attend their special staff at nine. I've marked it on the map on the front seat so that an idiot couldn't get lost, but you'll probably manage. I want you back with your patient in my office by four o'clock."

"Do you know if the patient's tractable? I'll be alone with him in the car and—"

"He's just a child, and I don't have time for details. Dr. Semminetti went up yesterday evening to bring him back, but there have been complications. He'll fill you in on the case. He talked to his mother in Paris yesterday. He's an old friend of the patient's family and so am I. Don't discuss this case with anyone. Thank God they've kept it out of the news up there. The boy's name is Stelgis Kara-Kash. Does that mean anything to you?"

"Of course. We used his textbook in genetics. Wasn't he nominated for a Nobel?"

"Twice, but he talked too much. This boy is his grandson. His mother is Dr. Sophia Kara-Kash, now a biologist at the University of Chicago—used to be here. She's on an exchange lectureship at Pasteur Institute. She's flying in from Paris and will be in my office at four. You be there with her son by four, too. It's three hours to Hanover, but allow yourself an extra hour. Better get started now."

"Yes, sir," I said, hoping to end the conversation, but he wasn't through with me.

"What's this other nonsense Falstein keeps telling me about your thinking of switching to neurology?"

I felt anger rising in me again. "Dr. Falstein gets some strange ideas about me at times," I said. "Don't you agree that he sometimes overevaluates his hunches?"

"I don't intend to lie here at four in the morning listening to a resident criticize a colleague. He tells me you have a way with adolescents; I can understand why. Have you thought about giving your last two years to child psychiatry? If this kid stays with us here, maybe we'll assign him to you. Think about that, if you feel abused. And if you wreck my new Mercedes, you'll be held financially liable. Good morning!"

My ears were still ringing as I took a shower, shaved and changed clothes, then got two Dexedrene tablets from my medical case, feeling abused and exhausted and overwhelmed by problems greater than a trip to Hanover State Hospital.

I began fingering the Dexedrene tablets in my jacket pocket as the solid little Mercedes purred its way into the Ramapos, thirty miles north of the bridge. As I passed the Anthony Wayne Recreation Area of Bear Mountain Park, from which I had departed only a few hours before with Margaret Bochmeir, I grimaced and tried to switch my thoughts to more pleasant things, but Karsloff had opened a bucket of worms that would wiggle through my consciousness until I resolved a problem I had not known existed until last evening. The truth struck me suddenly and I knew that Dr. Gustav Golm, who considered himself knowledgeable about human behavior, had become the victim of a family conspiracy now so obvious that a high school boy should have seen through it weeks ago.

Margaret Bochmeir is twenty-four, in the prime of feminine ripeness, with hair the color of ripe Indiana wheat and trusting blue eyes that are somewhat brightened by contact lenses. She is the only child of a former butcher who owns a chain of German delicatessens that are strategically located in shopping centers throughout Long Island and Westchester and Rockland counties. Although her family maintains a $250,000 estate in Riverdale, Margaret has a room at Hadley Hall. Until last evening I had wondered only vaguely at this show of independence, admiring her for her desire to live near her patients. It was now obvious that her motivation had nothing to do with devotion to duty: Margaret and her parents had simply taken a logical, practical course toward their goal. They had set out to bring a doctor into their family circle. It had probably started with parental guidance toward a career in nursing at one of the world's great medical centers, which has an attending staff of 988 physicians, a house staff of 466 interns, residents and fellows, and more than a thousand medical, dental and paramedical students.

Prior to the night that she'd spent in my bed at Butler Tower, she had played the waiting game, sharing her charms among a number of young doctors, including an oral surgeon, a recently certified radiologist, a resident in urology and an assistant professor of public health.

There is always a challenge to an aggressive male in

such a situation and I had walked into the Bochmeir trap without a thought about possible future complications. In a moment of weakness, I had asked Margaret how she would like to live in Indianapolis, telling her that I'd probably open my practice there. "Oh, Gustav, I'd love it!" she had cried, and from that moment she had assumed that we were engaged. She dropped the competition immediately and went meekly and eagerly to my apartment. Two weeks later, lying on a blanket in Bear Mountain Park, she had finished the Chianti, then started to cry, looking at me with an expression that any medical student could have diagnosed at twenty yards. My defenses were alerted for the first time and it seemed incredible to me that an R.N. with almost four years of clinical experience and generations of cautious, practical Schleswig-Holstein ancestors could have been so careless. I felt exactly as General Eisenhower must have felt when informed of the surprise attack at the Battle of the Bulge.

"What's wrong, for goodness sake?" I asked, dreading the answer.

"I—I think we're in trouble, Gustav," she sobbed.

"My God, you don't mean you haven't been taking the pill?"

"I've been afraid of them since that last report from A.D.A."

"But it's only been two weeks. The chances are only—"

"But I'm always regular. I never wanted it to happen this way. Please don't be angry with me."

It took me three hours after we got back to Hadley Hall to convince her that the probability of pregnancy was only slight, but I had not convinced myself. I began sorting out the options now open to me. I could marry Margaret immediately, making her and her parents very happy and guaranteeing a secure future for myself and what would likely be a large family. But as I thought of Bertha Bochmeir, Margaret's mother, who now weighed close to 250 pounds and suffered a severe genu valgum that probably would in time afflict her daughter, it seemed out of the question.

With two years of my residency completed, I could go into practice at once, perhaps in Alaska, where *Medical Economics* had reported only one psychiatrist for 150,000 population. As I thought of the subzero temperatures and the long arctic nights, I also discarded that option.

If I told Margaret that I was already married to an Indiana girl, it might be easier to convince her that the most practical road to travel would be toward the abortion unit at the Gynecology Pavilion. But I realized I couldn't live with such a lie. There had to be a solution that wouldn't hurt other people too much—there always had been—and I would simply have to wait until I found it, if nature didn't resolve the problem for us.

I turned off beyond Monticello, stopping for breakfast in a diner at the second town I came to. On impulse, I decided to call Margaret before she left for duty. She answered on the second ring.

"Oh, Gustav! How sweet of you to call. You knew I was frightened and upset last night. You're always so thoughtful. But everything's all right this morning. I knew the moment my cramps woke me just before six. I—I wouldn't have minded having a baby now. Really—but I knew you were upset. We have a lot of time to think about a family. I just talked with Mamma. We've been planning a surprise for you—can you come for dinner tonight?"

"Not a chance," I said, feeling a heavy burden lifting from my shoulders. "I'm up in the Catskills, going to Hanover State Hospital for Dr. Karsloff. Don't know when I'll get back. See you tomorrow. I hung up quickly, paid my check and went back to the car.

I drove slowly on the road that meandered through the valley, reducing speed so that I wouldn't arrive too early. With one problem resolved, I began thinking of another. It was obvious that Dr. Falstein had been discussing me with Dr. Karsloff. I resented him revealing information that he'd learned in a doctor-patient relationship, especially to our chief of service.

Falstein is in his middle thirties, only a few years my senior, but he is one of those doctors who seems to have been born old. He's my preceptor in psychiatry and has the same relationship with three other residents. We go to him weekly for psychotherapy sessions, a requirement for all residents. Falstein is a bachelor, a rather shy, gentle person, with brown eyes that can cloud with hurt at the slightest provocation. Although he appears confident with me, I know that I have a knack for getting under his skin when he tries to probe too deeply into my personal affairs. When he does, I always turn him off by restating my thoughts about switching my specialty from psychiatry to neurology.

As I remembered our last few sessions, it occurred to me that Falstein seemed more interested in my relationship with Margaret Bochmeir than with any of the other nurses I had dated. This was probably due to Margaret's assignment as charge nurse on the locked twelfth floor, where many of his acute patients were hospitalized.

I reached Hanover at eight-thirty and turned off the highway at a sign that pointed toward the hospital. As I passed through its wide, arched front gate, it suddenly occurred to me that I still had a major problem to resolve.

It was obvious that Margaret and her parents now took our marriage for granted. A possible solution struck me suddenly as I turned into the circle that fronted the Administration Building and parked in the area reserved for doctors. Since the Bochmeirs' primary goal seemed to be bringing a physician into their family cycle, why not find them a doctor who would be even more attractive? I had a possible candidate: he was an associate professor of psychiatry, with good prospects for an early professorship, and was highly respected throughout the medical community, both as a teacher and clinician. Promoting the marriage would certainly be a challenge, what with Falstein's shyness and Oscar Bochmeir's prejudices, but I hadn't given the last two years of my life to the study of human behavior and motivation for nothing.

I was smiling as I walked up the steps and entered the Administration Building, suddenly feeling in control of my own destiny again.

Chapter Two

Dr. Theodore Semminetti, like his classmate Karsloff, is in his early forties, a small, fastidious, carefully groomed man who seems to wear a chronic expression of disapproval. He has a sallow complexion, prematurely gray hair, a short mustache and long, thin nose, which seems to be constantly sniffing some objectionable odor. He is respected in the profession and is considered an expert on the affective psychoses. He gives a limited amount of his time to treating private patients in a Midtown office: many of us have wondered why he limits this part of his practice to women.

Dr. Semminetti was sitting in the superintendent's waiting room when I entered a few minutes before nine. He looked up from his magazine, met my eyes briefly, then returned to his reading without greeting me. Then he rose abruptly and stood at the window to my left, staring out over the flower beds. He stood there for some time, stroking his mustache, then turned suddenly to face me.

"May I ask what you are doing here this morning, Dr. Golm?"

"Dr. Karsloff sent me," I replied. "I'm supposed to attend their special staff conference this morning and take the patient back to the institute."

His body seemed to tense even more and it was obvious that he was finding it difficult to control his rage. "I

17

resent your intrusion into this case, Golm—that Leon would interject a stranger into the situation when he knows very well that—"

The door of the superintendent's office opened and Dr. Donaldson came in, smiling apologetically. He was a large, portly man who lectured frequently at the institute. "I'm sorry to have kept you waiting so long, gentlemen," he said, "but I've been on the phone for the past twenty minutes with Dr. Karsloff. He wanted to talk to you, too, Dr. Semminetti, but was called to an emergency. He asked me to explain why our staff feels it wouldn't be wise for you to become involved with our patient at this time—"

"Somebody certainly owes me an explanation! I drove up here late yesterday on instructions from the patient's mother. When I arrived, I was denied access to the patient, whom I have known since birth, and no one would explain why. The commissioner is certainly going to hear about it. Of that you can be sure."

"I'm terribly sorry, Ted, I wasn't notified that you were here. Dr. Harris, who has had the case, was in intensive care, dealing with an acute suicidal patient. When the patient learned of your presence, he asked that he not have to see you. He's been highly disturbed, and Dr. Morgan, our clinical director, felt that the boy should not be—"

"And may I ask why the mother was not notified of her son's admission until yesterday noon?"

"He came to us as a John Doe, Doctor. We had to place him under Pentothal late Friday evening in order to learn his identity. We tried to reach Dr. Kara-Kash in Paris, but she was away for the weekend."

"It's preposterous to say that Stelgis would not want to see me. I've visited him weekly at camp, missing only last week, when I had to attend a meeting in California. We've always had a warm relationship. I'd like the details of his admission now."

"Our staff meeting is waiting to get under way," the superintendent said, "and we should get over there immediately. Our information on the patient is far from complete, but you'll hear all we have as it is presented. I'd like you to withdraw to our observation station when the patient is brought in, Ted. There's a one-way mirror and a sound system. We shouldn't upset the patient if we can avoid it. Shall we go?"

Dr. Semminetti continued to pout and fume as we crossed the lawn toward their new Admission-Diagnostic Center, walking apart from us, making sure we knew just how offended he felt.

"Dr. Karsloff had some very nice things to say about you, Dr. Golm," the superintendent said as we approached the building. "He believes you have a bright future. He's seldom wrong about his residents."

"My God," I said in surprise, "he's never mentioned anything like that to me. He usually refers to me as that irresponsible German dunderhead who never conforms to anything he doesn't—"

"Don't take Leon's sarcasm too seriously. When you've known him as long as I have, you'll learn that he never treats his favorites with less than verbal abuse and extra duties."

We entered the building and walked down a brightly polished corridor to the staff room, where doctors and other staff members were seated around the conference table. Dr. Donaldson introduced us, then took his chair at the head of the table.

"Sorry to have delayed you, ladies and gentlemen, but I was on the telephone. We have only one case this morning, but it's a most unusual one. We have not had nearly enough time for a complete workup, and our history is patchy, but I must congratulate Dr. Harris and Miss Holmes for the information they've obtained. I would suggest that when the patient is brought in for questioning you refrain from pressing him too hard. Will you present the case, Dr. Harris?"

Dr. Harris was in his middle thirties, a physician and psychiatrist who had lectured at the institute.

"The patient is a twelve-year-old white male, in excellent physical health, who appears much older, both physically and intellectually. He was remanded to us by the county judge, from the Hanover Community Hospital, last Thursday for evaluation and recommendations. He was taken to the community hospital by the police early Wednesday morning from the Barkus Hotel and

19

Restaurant Supply Company, located at the edge of town, after being found there by Mr. Barkus. The boy was locked inside his refrigerated meat room, lying naked on a wood packing case and was said to be in a stuporous, near comatose state when discovered. It is assumed that he slipped into the building just before closing time, hiding until the employees had gone for the day. He is known to have been at the place once before as a member of a detail sent to get supplies for the boys' camp where he had been placed by his mother late in June. The camp is four miles from Hanover, in the mountains.

"Mr. Barkus stated that Stelgis—the patient—had been taking his temperature rectally at half-hour intervals, recording it on a paper found beside him. Barkus called the police, who took Stelgis to the local hospital, where he was given hot liquids and placed under an electric blanket. The last recorded temperature, made by the boy at 4 A.M., was ninety-seven point six degrees Fahrenheit. His temperature was normal two hours after his arrival at the hospital. Fortunately, the meat-room temperature is maintained at about forty degrees, well above freezing.

"One incident at the hospital in town bears mentioning. The patient's clothes had been hung in the closet of his room and his valuables had been taken from him, but he apparently had other money hidden in his clothes. When the security guard apprehended him trying to slip out through the hospital's back entrance at 10:30 P.M., he offered the guard ten dollars to let him pass, saying he had to catch the last bus to New York to meet his mother. He refused to give his name or any explanation of his bizarre behavior.

"It was presumed that he had come from one of the many boys' camps located in this vicinity. The sheriff's office made a thorough check at each camp, but there was no one missing or unaccounted for. The judge had no other recourse but to send him to us. Perhaps this would be a good point for Miss Holmes to present the information she obtained from Mr. Carter, director of the camp."

The social worker read from a prepared report. "Mr. Carter informed me that the patient can imitate his mother's signature almost flawlessly. Stelgis, the patient, apparently typed a letter on his mother's stationery and had it mailed from New York to Mr. Carter. It stated that she would be in New York Wednesday and that her son should be permitted to come to the city by bus to remain with her through Thursday. The thermometer used by the patient was taken from the camp's nursing office.

"Mr. Carter said that the mother had come to the camp with her son, that she was a reserved, shy woman, who seemed deeply interested in her child's welfare. She described him as precocious, excitable and apt to be domineering. She said that she would be in Paris for the month of July and asked to be kept informed of her son's behavior, saying that it was his first time away from her and that she hoped he could benefit from association with other boys his age.

"Stelgis did not make a good camp adjustment, maintaining a superior attitude that was resented by his camp mates. Mr. Carter stated that despite his size and obvious strength, he became the victim of another boy—described as the camp bully—who continued to taunt and ridicule him and finally slapped him, daring him to fight, but Stelgis simply turned his back and walked away. Mr. Carter heard of the incident and called Stelgis to his office, telling him that he would never be accepted by the other boys until he proved to them that he wasn't a coward. Stelgis told him that he was only afraid of hurting the other boy, as he'd hurt a boy in Chicago, and had promised his mother that he wouldn't fight again. Mr. Carter told him that he had a right to fight when he was attacked. Next day at the lake, the other boy, who comes from the Bronx and is named Anthony Peroni, challenged him. Stelgis gave him a terrible beating, then dragged him into the water and might have drowned him if the other boys hadn't intervened.

"Following this incident, Stelgis became the camp leader. He made the most of his new role, according to Mr. Carter, becoming aggressive and domineering. He said that his intelligence was at the genius level, that he was in a special class for exceptional children at the University of Chicago. He then stated that he could withstand cold better than any other living person and that he could prove it scientifically. This apparently explains his adventure in the meat locker. I guess that about covers all that I learned."

"Thank you, Miss Homes," Dr. Harris said. "Upon his arrival here the patient remained unco-operative, refused to give his name or any other information. Late Friday afternoon, as a last resort, we placed him under Pentothal for questioning. He responded quite well. He gave us his name, the name of his camp and the name of his mother. When we asked for the name of his father, he made a very bizarre statement—" Dr. Harris glanced at the faces about the table, watching our reactions as he said, "The patient said that his father has been dead for eighteen thousand years, that he was an Ice Age man. When questioned after recovering from the drug, he was again unco-operative and refused to elucidate further. However, Mr. Watkins, who is in charge of our receiving service, seems to have developed a good relationship with the patient. Will you tell us about your relationship, John?"

The male nurse smiled. "He's an extraordinary kid, for sure. We seemed to hit it off well from the beginning, but I soon learned that he was deliberately setting up a relationship that he could exploit. He finally told me that he had some valuable papers hidden in an envelope under a loose board in his cabin at camp, then said he would give me ten dollars if I would get it and his other things. I told him I would do it, but I didn't want to be paid. Mr. Carter accompanied me to the cabin. We found his hiding place, but there was nothing in it. Stelgis seemed very upset when I told him this. Later, he opened up and I learned quite a bit about him. He said that he and his mother usually spend the summer in his grandfather's old apartment, which is near the American Museum of Natural History, of which his grandfather had been a trustee, that he knew most of the curators there and that he could go where he pleased when he visited the museum. He couldn't have made it up, or learned what he told me about their research from reading. I—"

A loud sniffing came from Dr. Semminetti, sitting at my left, and it gained the superintendent's attention. "We are most fortunate to have Dr. Semminetti with us today," he said. "He's an old and dear friend of the Kara-

Kash family. Perhaps he will fill us in on the boy's background?"

Dr. Semminetti rose from his chair and stood silently for several seconds, stroking his mustache, scowling. "I must ask to be excused," he said. "Since I have been refused access to the patient and Dr. Golm has been given the responsibility of returning him to New York, I see no point in giving you information that you will eventually receive through normal channels. Good morning, ladies and gentlemen."

He walked to the door, opened it, then turned about facing us. "Has it occurred to you people that Stelgis could have been leading you down the garden path? When you've known him as long as I have, you'll know that he is quite capable of it. Of one thing I'm certain— he's not psychotic, as many of you are now assuming. He does not have a high regard for psychiatry or psychiatrists, nor did his famous grandfather." He went through the door and would have slammed it had the door check not interfered.

Dr. Donaldson waited for a moment, smiling, then said, "I fear we've offended Dr. Semminetti, but it couldn't be helped." He turned to Dr. Morgan, the clinical director, who sat on his right. "Dr. Morgan, you had the fortune or misfortune of having worked in his grandfather's lab when you were doing your fellowship at the medical center. Could you tell us what you know about the family history?"

"Dr. Stelgis Kara-Kash was certainly one of the world's great biologists and geneticists, leaving a body of work that ranks with the best. He was nominated twice for the Nobel and passed over each time. He was a total egotist, without tact, and seldom opened his mouth when the press was near without putting his foot in it. His wife died when the patient's mother was quite young. He adored the child and brought her regularly to his lab, where he cooked outlandish dishes for them over a Bunsen burner. Losing the Nobel the second time broke his heart, I suspect, and he died a couple of years later. His wife had been in and out of that private sanitarium in Connecticut before her death. It was assumed that she was psychotic. Knowing her husband, it was not difficult to understand why. I know little about the daughter's life; I left the medical center when she was still a student.

"She's a biologist at the University of Chicago," the superintendent said, "and a brilliant one, according to Dr. Karsloff, who also told us that our patient was born out of wedlock when the mother was still a student. Do you have other information, Dr. Harris? If not, would you give us your conclusions?"

"I would not attempt to make a classification on the information we have, except to say that this is a very troubled little boy. Despite what Dr. Semminetti said, I would not rule out a latent psychosis. If it should develop, I suspect it will take a paranoid course. I'll be most interested in learning what happens to the patient in the years ahead."

"Thank you, Dr. Harris. Perhaps we should bring the patient in now. I'm sure you gentlemen will be interested in meeting him."

The nurse went out of the room and returned shortly with the patient, one of the most unusual children I have seen. He was short, with a solid mesomorphic body. Looking at his well-muscled shoulders and torso, I could well imagine his ability to defend himself among boys his age. He had a square face, which showed the first fuzz of what would someday be a heavy black beard, matched by very thick eyebrows and lashes. Showing not the slightest trace of nervousness or fear as he took the chair beside the superintendent, he seemed only curious as he glanced at his audience. His prognathous jaw and chin were thrust aggressively forward, but his brown eyes seemed to be laughing at us.

"Thank you for coming to our meeting, Stelgis," Dr. Donaldson said. "We've all been anxious to meet you. We won't take much of your time. Dr. Golm there in the last chair to your left is here to take you to meet your mother in New York."

"I do not intend to answer any of your questions," the boy said, then looked at me, meeting my eyes. When he continued to try to stare me down, I winked at him and he smiled, hesitated, then his left eyelid moved ever so slightly. For some reason I felt flattered.

"You told Dr. Harris that you can withstand cold better than anyone else, Stelgis. How about that? Were you having a little fun at his expense?"

"My teachers tell me I have a wild imagination. Who knows what I might say when drugged? If I'm going to meet Sophia, why don't we go now? I won't answer any questions."

"Oh, come now, let's not be in such a rush. You've had an extraordinary adventure, and we simply want to—"

The boy turned to stare up at the superintendent. "Have you had a physical examination recently?" he asked. "I'll bet you're a hundred pounds overweight, that your cholesterol is at least five hundred. There are five cigarette butts in your ashtray, and you're ready to light another. You need a doctor and—"

"All right, that's enough of that. We're not here to talk about my health problems and—"

I coughed suddenly, then said, as Dr. Donaldson looked at me, "Perhaps we should be heading back to New York soon. If the nurse and Stelgis will get his things and take them to the white Mercedes parked in front of the Administration Building, I'll meet them there in fifteen minutes."

"I think that's a good idea. Good-bye, Stelgis, and don't think too badly of us."

The boy ignored him and followed the nurse out of the room.

"Any comments, ladies and gentlemen?"

"I wouldn't rule out a psychosis," one of the younger doctors said. "His rigidity, superiority and confidence are equal to that of any adult paranoid I have on my service. I think he's going through something that's far more serious than adolescent fantasy. I'd suspect, at his age, it could develop into a full-blown schizophrenia."

"It's quite remarkable, this boy's resemblance to his grandfather," Dr. Morgan said. "For a moment, it was almost as though the old man himself was sitting there before us. I worked in his research lab for several months, and there wasn't a moment I was there that I didn't live in fear of him."

"Could you tell us how he lost the Nobel twice, Dr. Morgan?" another young doctor asked.

The clinical director looked at the superintendent.

"Perhaps we can discuss it after this meeting is over? We—"

"No, we'd all like to hear about it."

Dr. Morgan smiled. "As I said before, he was totally lacking in tact. His first nomination came when we were having segregation problems throughout the South. A professor of anthropology at the University of Pennsylvania named Brodermen—a southerner—had made a public statement that most Negroes were not up to the challenge of higher education. A reporter asked Dr. Kara-Kash what he thought. The old man said that it could only have been made by a congenital idiot, posing as a pedagogue, that all races are born equal and then shaped by cultural pressures, that if we could bring a baby from the Ice Age and place it in an average American family it would grow up and not be intellectually different from its siblings, and that it takes more than eighteen thousand years to change a human brain by the evolutionary process. The professor from Pennsylvania picked it up and an angry dialogue developed between them that went on in the press for months, doing credit to neither."

"Yes, I remember that one," the superintendent said, "and I couldn't agree with you more."

"The old man's statement following his second nomination was even more indiscreet. An astute reporter, looking for colorful copy, asked him what he'd learned about genetics from his years of research. The old man said that doctors and the Judeo-Christian ethic were helping mankind commit genetic suicide, that we should immediately sterilize all carriers of dangerous genes—diabetics, mental defectives, schizophrenics and others. It brought both the medical and the religious community down on him. Many biologists might have secretly agreed with him, but they couldn't let it pass with Hitler's ideas so fresh in the public mind. The media picked it up and it went over the wires world-wide. I still think they would have had to give the prize to the old man had he lived because his work changed world thinking."

"Any questions?"

"Yes, I have one," I said. "Do you know anything about who this boy's father might have been?"

"No," Dr. Donaldson said. "I guess that about winds it up, ladies and gentlemen. Thank you for coming."

Dr. Donaldson walked with me to the car, where both nurse and patient were waiting with the boy's belongings, which we placed in the trunk. The nurse offered to shake hands with the boy, who walked around him and entered the car.

The superintendent took my arm and guided me to the sidewalk.

"Keep me informed," he said. "I hope you get a chance to work with him. Don't take too seriously the things you heard in our meeting. I've dealt with many adolescents, and I'm almost certain that this child is not psychotic. He needs help, though, and your first goal should be to gain his trust and friendship. And don't feel too badly about Dr. Semminetti's display of temper. Leon says he's always been extremely jealous of his relationship with the patient's mother. Have a good trip back to New York."

My patient remained silent as I backed out and drove slowly toward the front gate, where I stopped before turning onto the highway.

"Is there anything special you'd like to do, Stelgis, before we head for New York? We've plenty of time to spare." When he continued to be silent, I pressed the gas pedal gently and moved through the gate, turning toward town and the quickway.

"I thought you were in such a hurry to get back," he said suspiciously. "What did he say your name is?"

"Golm. My friends call me Gus. Actually, we have some time to kill. I just wanted to get out of the gloomy place. How about you?"

He looked away from me, ignoring my question. I increased our speed, pretending indifference.

"Could we drive out to my camp?" he asked.

"Sure, but you'll have to direct me."

"Turn right at the next corner. It's four miles straight west."

I made no effort at conversation as we drove into the mountains, but whistled softly.

"What kind of doctor are you?"

"I enter my third-year residency in psychiatry this month."

He thought for a moment, then said, "Psychiatry is not a scientific discipline. Most of what Freud said was nonsense. That's what my grandfather wrote. He said that most psychiatrists are more mixed up than their patients and—"

"And that they miss few opportunities to speak for God when God is not readily available to speak for Himself?"

"Where did you read that one? I've been making a collection of Grandfather's quotes. She has all of his papers in bound volumes, but I never read that one."

"What would you say if I told you I'd made it up?"

"Did you?"

"Yes."

'If you feel that way about psychiatrists, why would you pick psychiatry as your specialty?"

"That's a good question. Maybe because, like your grandfather said, I'm a little mixed up myself. I think, though, that it was probably because I dislike psychiatry less than I dislike general medicine and surgery."

"That's funny."

"Not really. Freud said one thing that was far from being nonsense: he said that someday biologists would find biological and genetic factors to explain mental illness. And that's what's happening today."

"That's what *she* says."

"Who?"

"Sophia. She's been doing a lot of research with rhesus monkeys."

"What kind of research?"

"My grandfather believed that schizophrenia is due to both genetic and physical factors—not social ones. She believes that, too, and is going to prove it with her monkeys."

It occurred to me that he referred to his mother only as "she," "her" or "Sophia"; he had not once used the word "mother." To keep the conversation going, I said, "Many of the things Freud predicted are now happening. Have you heard about the drug lithium, which is now being used to control hypermanics?"

"Sure. You can't be around Uncle Ted very long without hearing about lithium. He claims he was using it for manics a year before that Australian published his paper on it. Lithium is almost like common table salt."

"Tell me a little more about your mother's work with her monkeys," I said.

"Why don't you ask her? You'll be meeting her when we get to New York." He turned abruptly away from me to stare out the window.

I pretended to ignore him and turned on the radio. A violin concerto was in progress. Stelgis listened a moment, then said, "I'll bet you can't name that piece of music."

It was my favorite of all classical music, the Brahms "Violin Concerto," but I listened a moment, then suggested that it sounded like something by Tchaikovsky.

He snorted loudly, looking and acting his age for the first time, then correctly identified the piece.

"You're amazing, Stelgis," I said. "When I was your age, I thought the world began and ended in Bordentown, Indiana. You know a lot about medicine, psychiatry, music, and you have the vocabulary of a college graduate. How have you managed to accumulate so much knowledge at your age?"

He frowned and turned away from me again, and I knew for certain that I should avoid questions about his personal life. I changed the subject abruptly.

"This is a terrific little car, isn't it?"

"We've got a new BMW," he said.

"Does your mother let you drive it?"

He hesitated, then grinned and said, "Not anymore." When I failed to question him, he added, "She used to let me drive it when I was with her out on country roads. But last January I slipped out in it alone. The police picked me up when I was on the Midway in front of the university. I promised her I wouldn't drive it again until I was old enough to get a learner's permit."

"And you're the kind who keeps his promises."

He snorted gleefully again. "And I don't really know much about music," he said. "It's just that Brahms' 'Violin Concerto' is her favorite piece of music. She plays it all the time when she's in the dumps—that one and Tchaikovsky's 'Sixth Symphony.' "

" 'The Pathétique,' " I said. "That's one of my favorites, too."

"You have to turn off and go up the next road," he said. "The camp is almost at the top of the mountain. You'll have to park at the fence."

I drove slowly up the winding gravel road. As I heard and felt the stones popping against the fenders, I knew that I would have some explaining to do to Dr. Karsloff.

The road ended at a small parking area where a fence separated the camp from the road. There was a large stone house to our left, flanked by a row of log cabins which were built in a half circle around a roofed pavilion that probably served as a mess hall and shelter during rainy weather. I parked close to the fence, under the shade of a giant oak, and turned off the motor.

We waited silently for several moments, then I said, "How long do you think you'll be gone, Stelgis?"

Again, I'd taken him by surprise. He continued to stare out the window, then faced me, a questioning expression on his face.

"You mean you don't intend to go with me?" he asked.

"Why should I?"

"I thought you were sent to be my guard or something."

"Whatever made you think that?"

"They've sure been keeping me locked up for almost a week. Didn't they tell you I'm crazy?"

"Of course not. No one has thought that. Take as much time as you need as long as you get back by noon. It's almost eleven now."

He opened the door and got out, started to speak, hesitated, then turned and went through the gate toward the cabins, where a ball game seemed to be in progress. There was something about his posture as he went up the rather steep incline that was both sad and brave. I suddenly felt affection and pity for him as he went to face his camp mates. That he was a very lonely child I was certain, and I suspected that there were logical explanations for his behavior. It seemed obvious that he had spent most of his life among adults and had become skilled in manipulating them. I agreed with Dr. Harris that he was a very troubled boy, beginning to act out a fantasy life that, if not interrupted, could lead to serious problems. What he needed most was an opportunity to form a relationship with an adult male who might in time become a surrogate for a father he had never known. He also felt defensive and unsure of himself among peers and needed to live among them long enough to develop the social skills he seemed to have missed. Perhaps a good boy's boarding school with an understanding staff, might be a wise recommendation to make to his mother.

There was a warm breeze blowing through the open windows. I adjusted the bucket seat, then lay back, totally relaxed, knowing that Dr. Karsloff would expect me to make recommendations—which would, of course, depend entirely upon her attitude toward her son and her willingness to admit that he had serious problems. Remembering the things about her imperious and domineering father, I suspected that she would not be too different. Thinking of the many hard, aggressive women scientists I'd know during my years of medical school and training, I doubted that she would accept recommendations from any male doctor, especially a second-year resident. I yawned and closed my eyes.

Chapter Three

I woke suddenly from a strange dream, not moving, uncertain of my whereabouts until I recognized the stone house and cabins. It was noon and there was no sign of my patient. Had I been too eager to win his confidence and trust? I decided to give him another ten minutes before going to look for him.

I again closed my eyes, then jumped guiltily as Stelgis' face appeared in the window.

"My God, where did you come from?" I asked.

"I've been back about twenty minutes."

"Why didn't you wake me?"

"You said we had an hour to spare and you sure looked like you needed sleep. I just sat down outside and waited, listening to you moan and groan. You must have had some dream."

"Get in," I said gruffly. "We'd better be on our way." When he continued to grin impishly, I asked, "What's so darned funny?"

"You talk a lot in your sleep. Just like her when she has bad dreams."

"Like who?"

"Sophia. She dreams a lot too."

I changed the subject. "How did you make out at camp?"

His expression changed quickly to a frown. When he didn't answer, I repeated it. "He had another fight Saturday and they sent him home, but I know where he lives," he said. "If he has my things, he's going to pay." When I tried to question him further, he said, "I don't want to talk now."

I turned around and drove slowly back on a road that had become tacky from the hot sun. As we turned toward Hanover, I asked if he was hungry.

"Sure. Can we stop at McDonald's? It's on our way."

McDonald's was on the main highway at the south edge of town. When Stelgis insisted upon paying the check, I let him and it seemed to please him, but I could feel his tension mounting as I hit a steady speed toward the quickway. He continued to talk—mostly, I suspect, because he feared what he had to face when we reached New York. I didn't try to interrupt or let him know that I was especially interested, so I learned quite a bit that he might not otherwise have told me.

He and his mother lived in a new high-rise apartment building close to the University of Chicago. He was in a special class for expectional children where each student was allowed to progress at his own pace. He was now doing work at a third-year high school level and finding it easy. His special interest was life sciences, and he talked knowledgeably about the prospects of human engineering. He said Sophia taught biology at the medical school but hated it and wanted to give all her time to research. She had published several papers and also had completed some of his grandfather's work, publishing it under both of their names. Uncle Ted came frequently to visit them in Chicago. Without prompting, he asked if Uncle Ted had returned from Hanover to New York last night.

"Why did you refuse to see him while he was there?" I asked. "He was hurt and upset. It wasn't very kind of you."

"Uncle Ted gets upset easily," he replied, then changed the subject. "What was it like where you grew up as a kid, Gus?" he asked, using my name for the first time.

"Like it was in most rural county-seat towns in the Midwest. We had the river and lots of lakes for fishing and swimming. We hunted rabbits and quail in season. There were several boys my exact age and we grew up together, more like brothers than friends."

34

"Did you have a nickname?"

"I was called Doc from the time I can remember because my father and grandfather were both doctors."

"Didn't they ever call you other funny names?"

"As I think about it, they did call me Moose when I was in first grade."

"Why Moose?"

"My grandfather was alive then, and most of his patients were farmers who often paid his fees in small change from the egg money. He threw the change into an empty pill bottle, and I was allowed to go through it and keep the bull-moose nickels. The kids found out and started calling me Moose, but it didn't last long."

"Did other kids have funny names?"

"Sure, all of them had nicknames. There was Cow Carr, Boom-Boom Boggs, who had a double-barrelled shotgun that sometimes shot twice when he pulled only one trigger, Plug Hayes, who got sick from chewing his father's tobacco, and lots of others."

"Didn't it make them angry?"

"Why should it have?"

"Know what the kids at school started calling me?"

"What?"

"Monk and Chimp. Do you think I look like a monkey, Gus?"

"Of course not. You're going to break some nice girl's heart one of these days."

He snorted, blushing. "I got into a lot of fights over those names, until I promised her I wouldn't fight anymore. Do you suppose they called me that because I talked a lot in class about her research with monkeys?"

"That's it, of course," I reassured him. "Nicknames are usually symbols of affection," I said.

"They suddenly stopped calling me names. I think she talked to the teacher, and he talked to the kids about it."

He remained silent for several miles, digesting what I'd said, but I could feel his anxiety growing as we headed east. He touched my arm suddenly and said, "What are they going to do with me when we get to New York, Gus?"

"They're not going to do anything to you, Stelgis, except maybe give you a few tests and try to learn why you locked yourself in that meat room. You have to admit that looks like pretty strange behavior."

"So—do you think I'm psychotic?"

"I know you're not. All of us at your age had experiences that were just as strange to adults. My father didn't believe I'd amount to anything when I grew up and didn't hesitate to tell me so. He still doesn't believe I'll amount to much, not since I went into psychiatry."

"What kind of experiences did you have?"

I smiled suddenly, remembering one. "One Sunday I went home with Hubert Carr to their farm. His family was visiting in town. Hubert and I made a big parachute, using his mother's best sheets that were hanging in the summerhouse to dry. I dared Hubert to go first, and that's the way he got his name of Cow Carr."

"What happened?"

"He went off the peak of the barn roof. It was in late March and there was a big pile of soft cow manure directly below him. He went in up to his armpits. Took me a long time to dig him out with a pitchfork. We were trying to wash the sheets when his family came home and caught us. Hubert got his licking on the spot; I got mine when I got home."

"Didn't the chute work at all?"

"Until about halfway down and our knots came untied."

"Oh, I wish I could have seen it."

"Would you like to tell me about your experience in the meat room, Stelgis?"

"No. I want to think about what I'm going to tell her when I see her."

He remained silent as we crossed Long Mountain Parkway and turned down Palisades toward the bridge. As we approached the Jersey line, a beeper began to sound in the car's glove compartment. I opened it to find Dr. Karsloff's beeper under his service manual. The call had to be from him.

As I left the parkway and drove toward a filling station and public phone, the boy looked at me questioningly, an anxious expression returning to his face.

"It's from the medical center," I said. "I have to call in. One beep at a time means contact the center, two beeps mean get there as quickly as you can. Most of the attending physicians and all chiefs of service have them.

"That's neat," the boy said.

I parked by the booth and entered it to dial Dr. Karsloff's Centrex number at the institute. Miss Thomas, his secretary, put me through at once.

"Just where in the hell have you been, Golm? I've been trying to raise you for the past two hours. They said you left up there around eleven."

"I took the patient out to his camp, and we stopped to eat. We're at Orangeburg, just out of the mountains."

"We've got a problem. The boy's mother won't get in until morning. She only had stand-by and got bumped by two State Department VIP's. What about the patient? I guess we'll just have to admit him at the institute until we can talk to Sophia."

"Oh, no," I said. "We can't do that!"

"Why the hell not?"

"I think it would be too traumatic for him. I've just gained his confidence and I wouldn't want him to believe I've been untruthful. I said—well, I told him that we would talk to his mother and she would decide about—"

"But what the hell are we going to do with him until she arrives?"

I thought for a moment, then said, "I have a two-room apartment. How about me keeping him tonight? He can sleep on my sofa and—"

"That's a good idea, Golm. I'll expect you to have some specific recommendations to offer Sophia. I suspect she probably needs help almost as much as her son does. I talked to her in Paris at noon, tried to calm her down a little. What happened up there?"

"They wouldn't let Dr. Semminetti talk to the boy, and he was plenty upset."

"Don't tell me what I already know! He came here with his feathers all ruffled, could hardly talk about it— doesn't believe you should become involved in the case. What does Donaldson think?"

"He doesn't believe the boy is psychotic, but he thinks he needs help. I have a gut feeling Stelgis should be separated from his mother for a while, but not as a patient at the institute. I think a good boarding school might be the answer. There are several around that take pride in their ability to deal with disturbed adolescents, but they cost money."

"Don't worry about that. Do you know how much money old Kara-Kash's textbooks still bring each year, and he left Sophia his forty years' accumulation of annuities in CREF-TIAA. She doesn't have to work another day of her life."

"What's she like?"

"I'll let you draw your own conclusions after you meet her. I wouldn't want to prejudice your thinking."

"In other words, we have a dual problem. From all I've learned, I'd guess she's another rigid female scientist—"

"With a face like a pickled quince and the instincts of a cobra?"

"Something like that."

"Well, Golm, I'll be interested in your reactions. Have my car here by five. I missed a lot of sleep because of you last night. I've got to run now."

"Oh, Dr. Karsloff—"

"What the hell is it now?"

"I missed my day off. I've got to meet with Dr. Kara-Kash, and I have duty scheduled for the Emergency Service again tomorrow. Could I possibly have tomorrow to—"

"Okay, take the day off, Golm." He hung up abruptly.

I returned to the car, proud of my resourcefulness.

"Your mother won't get in until tomorrow morning," I told the boy. "You're going to spend the night with me at my apartment. Maybe we can coax Yong Ha into cooking us some spareribs and bok choy."

"Who is Yong Ha?"

"He's a Korean friend who lives near me in Butler Tower. And he's some cook. Do you like oriental food?"

"Do I ever! Tell me about Yong Ha."

I told him about Yong's speech problem and my work with him as we drove toward the bridge. He listened with great interest. When I'd finished, he asked, "Does he explode only when he becomes suddenly angry or excited?"

"That's it. When he takes time to think, he can keep

38

control, but that's the problem. He hardly ever takes time to think. Got any ideas about what we might do?"

"I'd like to think about it," he said, hesitated, then added, "Gus it's only three. Do you think you'd have time to drive me down to our apartment on Central Park West? I want to pick up something. It'll only take a few minutes."

"Is it important to you?"

"Very important."

"Do you have a key?"

"Joe will let me in. He's our doorman."

"I guess we have the time. And we can go to that Chinese market on Third Avenue."

Stelgis touched my arm, grinning. "Gus, if Yong Ha only loses control when he's excited, his blood pressure must go up all of a sudden. She did a lot of research on blood pressure with her chimps. The instrument shop made her a small blood-pressure machine that continuously records the pressure. Maybe something like that could be made for Yong Ha, with an electronic monitor that could give him a little shock when his pressure shoots up suddenly. Wouldn't that make him stop and think?"

"It sure would. Why didn't I think of something like that? We have a man in our instrument shop who is a genius in electronics. I know he can make that kind of apparatus."

"Can you get Yong Ha to wear it?"

"Of course. He won't like it, but he'll do it if I ask him in the right way. You're going to like Yong, Stelgis."

"Oh, I know I will. Do you think I could stay with you long enough to see if it works?"

"We'll have to talk with your mother about that," I said as we pulled into the tollgate at the bridge.

Chapter Four

We took the West Side Highway down to Seventy-ninth Street and turned uptown on Central Park West.

"That's Joe in front of our building, trying to catch someone a cab," the boy said.

I made a U-turn at the corner and pulled in to park at the curb in front of an obese doorman who was standing in the street, a whistle in his mouth. He recognized the boy and came forward to greet him. "Hey, what are you doing here, Stelgis?" the man asked, frowning. "You just missed Dr. Semminetti. How's camp?"

"Sophia's coming in from Paris in the morning, Joe. I have to get something from the apartment. Will you let me in?"

"That's what they pay me for. Your friend had better stay in the car. This is a no-parking zone and the cops are mean these days."

"I'll be right back, Gus," the boy said, then followed the doorman into the imposing building through its double glass doors.

I listened to the radio as I waited, adding up certain facts in my mind. If Dr. Sophia Kara-Kash could afford to maintain an apartment in this building and keep another in a new high rise in Chicago, the expense of keeping her son in a good boys' boarding school shouldn't present any problems, but could he be placed in one during the vacation months? It was really her problem, I thought, and she would have to work it out.

The doorman came out from the building alone, followed by an elderly woman and her white poodle, helped her into a cab, then came over to talk to me.

"That Stelgis is quite a boy, isn't he?" I asked him as he leaned against the car and looked at me through the open window.

"Yeah, he sure as hell is, and a tricky one, too. He said you're a doctor at the medical center. Know Dr. Semminetti there?"

"Yes, I do. He's on our faculty. Why do you say that Stelgis is tricky?"

"When you know him as well as I do, you won't ask that question. He drives them half crazy when he's here during the summer."

"Drives who crazy?"

"His mother and old Doc Semminetti. He just takes off whenever the urge hits him and they go crazy waiting for him to come home."

"Where does he go?"

"Sometimes to the museum, sometimes down to Broadway at Midtown. I think he likes the peep-show machines in the arcade. I caught him at the door one time with some postcards from down there. I took them away from him before his mother could see them. She's some lady, and that kid's too much for her. And he drives Semminetti up the wall, which doesn't take much."

"I hope Dr. Semminetti was in a better mood today than he was when I left him this morning."

"He wasn't bad today, but you should have heard him raving Saturday when he got back from California."

"What happened?"

"He claimed someone was in his apartment while he was away. It probably was Stelgis. In fact, I'm sure it was, but I didn't tell Semminetti that."

"What makes you so sure? Stelgis has been in a hospital upstate since last Wednesday."

"It was on Sunday. I didn't see him, but Donovan, who works weekends, said he was here, and I know he has a key to Semminetti's apartment. There was another kid here to see Semminetti around noon today, shortly after he came home. I took him up to the apartment. Makes me wonder a little about the doc."

"What do you mean?"

"You know what I mean—old bachelors and boys. There's two of them kind in this building, but I never suspected old Doc until today."

"It probably was one of his patients," I said.

"This kid was no patient. He was a smart-ass from the Bronx. I know what I know, but I don't make it a habit talking out of school about people in my building."

"Look, Joe, I need to know about this kid. Stelgis is in deep trouble and I want to help him. He had some trouble with a kid at camp who was from the Bronx. I'll keep anything you tell me in confidence."

"Sorry, Doc, but I like my job here."

I removed a five-dollar bill from my pocket, then held it out to him. "Buy yourself a couple of drinks when you get off duty. Did this kid have anything with him when he arrived here?"

"Yeah, he had a brown envelope, now that I think about it, and he didn't have it when he came down, but he had two twenty-dollar bills. That's what made me think—"

"How could you know that?"

"Because he caught a taxi here and gave the driver a number up on Gun Hill Road, in the Bronx. The driver wouldn't take him until he showed him money, and he showed two twenties." He stopped talking as Stelgis came out of the building, looking disturbed and angry. He moved back to the curb, stopping in front of the boy. "Did you lock that door when you left, boy?"

Stelgis walked imperiously around the doorman and got into the car. "Get what you wanted?" I asked, turning left to go toward Third Avenue. When he remained silent, looking away from me, I said, "Did you also go to Dr. Semminetti's apartment? Joe says you have a key."

"Joe's the biggest liar in New York. You said we had to stop at some Chinese market."

"It's just off Third Avenue. We'll have to go over to Park and come back on Ninety-fifth. Remind me to call Yong Ha before we leave there. He doesn't know that he's cooking dinner."

We were silent as we drove to the market, but I was thinking, putting the pieces of information I'd gotten from Joe into place. It was quite possible that a boy with Stelgis' resourcefulness could have slipped out of camp and taken a bus to New York and back on Sunday. But why? I felt certain Joe had been truthful about the boy from the Bronx visiting Semminetti today, and I suspected the envelope contained the papers taken from Stelgis' hiding place under his cabin's floor.

Stelgis went with me into the market, where we bought the kind of ribs that aren't usually found in supermarkets, Chinese vegetables, the small shrimp that Yong Ha prefers, and some fresh noodles. As we were leaving, Stelgis pointed to a phone booth on the street. Yong Ha had been asleep when the phone rang and was in a foul nood.

"You're going to cook me and my friend some ribs and shrimp with lobster sauce for dinner tonight, okay?"

I waited for his verbal explosion to subside. "Somnoblitch," he cried, "all the time cook, cook for your mother—"

"That's enough," I interrupted. "I want you to meet us at the door in twenty minutes and take my friend up to my apartment while I deliver Dr. Karsloff's car to the institute. You be there, okay?"

He slammed the phone into its cradle.

Stelgis was listening through the open door behind me and grinned when I turned about. "Did he have another explosion?" he asked.

"It wasn't bad this time," I said. "It just takes him a little while to wake up. Oh, I forgot something." I turned back to the phone and dialed the number again. "Be sure and bring your wok," I said. "You took it home last time. And do you know if Dr. Helms is still working the emergency room nights?"

"No. In his room. Got a paper due. Who you bring for dinner?"

"Just wait and see," I said.

I heard a mild "somnoblitch" just before he hung up.

Yong Ha was waiting in front of the tower entranceway when we turned into the circle, scowling and squinting as he tried to identify my passenger. When he saw that it wasn't a female, a big grin spread over his face and he came forward to open the door.

"This is my friend Stelgis, Yong," I said, pushing the button that opened the trunk. "Will you help him with his things? He's staying with me tonight. I'll be back in a few minutes."

"Okay, Glom," he said. "Your woman called twice. She say you should call her soon as you can."

I watched them carry Stelgis's small camp locker, suitcase and typewriter to the doorway, then called them back to take the bag of food. I drove down to the institute, four blocks below the tower.

I put the car in Dr. Karsloff's reserved space, then went inside to leave the key with the security guard, who promised to take it to him before five. When I got back to the tower, I stopped off at the sixth floor and walked around to a corner apartment similar to my own. I pushed the button and Charley Helms opened the door a moment later, pen in hand, wearing only his shorts and bifocals.

"The dedicated Dr. Helms, I presume. And what's new today in the affective psychoses?"

"Up yours, Dr. Golm. Did you enjoy your day off in the Catskills?"

"Lovely, lovely. I saw by the duty roster that you're finally off emergency duty and back on the twelfth floor tomorrow. It will please you to know, I'm sure, that the grateful Dr. Karsloff is giving me tomorrow off, recognizing and rewarding me for my efforts in his volunteer programs."

"That bastard! Said I had to have my paper in by nine in the morning, or I'd be working in the post-mortem lab for the next month. He does have a way of making a point. What's on your mind? Finally found one you can't handle?"

"When do you have your next session with our preceptor?'

"He's graciously seeing me at eight tomorrow morning. We missed last week, and one adapts one's schedule to his, doesn't one?'

"Charley, I want you to do something for me. When you meet with Falstein in the morning, I want you to make him believe that Margaret Bochmeir is wild about

45

him. Don't lay it on too thick, but you know how to do it. And when you get up to the twelfth floor, I want you to make the same pitch to her. The brilliant Dr. Falstein is interested in her—he asks you a lot of questions about her, et cetera. You know the pitch."

"So the grazing in that pasture has run its course. I didn't think it would last *this* long. And what is the grateful Dr. Golm willing to do for his dear friend Dr. Helms?"

"I've got the best paper ever written on the affective psychoses, by a resident at Mass General, up in my room. I was saving it to use myself, but you can have it. How about it?"

"You've got a deal, but I need that paper now. I don't believe your scheme is going to work, though. Don't you get the feeling that our preceptor isn't interested in women?"

"He's interested, but scared. That's what I'm gambling on. Do a good job for me, pal."

"That I will. And I presume you'll reinforce what I say in your upcoming session with him?"

Stelgis and Yong Ha were giggling and talking up a storm when I entered the apartment. The makings of our dinner were on the counter by my stove, and the ribs were soaking up the marinade. I went to my desk, grabbed the paper and took it down to Dr. Helms, then went back to the apartment.

"When you want to eat, Glom?"

"Soon as I can have a shower and put on some fresh clothes. Has Stelgis told you about the prosthesis we're having made up for you?"

Yong Ha looked at me critically, questions forming in his mind. "What kind?"

"To help you cool down. God knows you need help, and soon. I talked to Dr. Vandermeer yesterday. He said you blew up at some poor old woman whose chest you were X-raying. If that happens when you're back in Hawaii in private practice you'll lose your license. What happened, for godsake?"

Yong Ha wet his lips, looking down at his shoes, a guilty expression on his face.

"Old somnoblitch move—every time move I shoot. Five times she move."

"You've got to expect that and think before you speak. This little apparatus we're having made up will work, won't it, Stelgis?"

"Sure it will, Yong."

"What it do?"

"It's just a miniature blood-pressure machine that can be strapped around your leg where it can't be seen. A tiny electronic device will give you a little shock when your blood pressure shoots up. You'll—"

Yong Ha's expression became more than scrutable. "No shock!" he cried and ran into the kitchen, followed by a rattling of pans, the sound of chopping and an explosion of obscenities. I met Stelgis' eye and winked, then went in to take my shower.

When I came out in fresh slacks and a sports shirt, a scotch and soda was waiting for me by my big chair. I was about to take my first sip as the phone rang. It was Margaret.

"Oh, Gus, I'm so glad you got back early. Mamma and Daddy insist upon your coming to dinner. You won't disappoint them, will you? They've been planning this surprise for a long time."

"I'm eating right now," I lied. "I'm tired and I have responsibilities here. I have the patient with me."

"Couldn't you come up later for a swim and the surprise? I'll pick you up. Please, Gus, it means so much to them. Couldn't—"

"All right,' I said, "but you'll have to pick me up. I guess Yong Ha can stay with my patient for an hour or so, but no longer. It's almost five now. Pick me up at seven."

Yong Ha and Stelgis were standing behind me, listening.

"Women, all the time women!" Yong Ha cried, shaking the empty wok, and he turned to run back to the kitchen.

When Stelgis started to follow Yong Ha, I lifted my hand. "I'll go get him in a minute. I think we'd better plan to have the device fit around his upper arm, don't you?" I was watching the door as I spoke.

The door flew open and Yong Ha came in. "No shock!" he said.

I went to him and put my arm about his shoulder. "Just take it easy."

"Okay, Glom."

"Good. How about me taking a nap now? Call me when it's ready."

I carried my drink to the bedroom, downed it in a few swallows, then lay down on the bed. They called me at six. The food was on the plates, and I poured a glass of wine for Yong Ha and myself, then got a Coke for Stelgis. It was a meal to remember and nothing was left when we had finished.

"Don't you think Yong's the best cook ever, Stelgis?" I asked, winking.

"He's even better than Don the Beachcomber," he said. "You should see that junk they shoved at us in camp. You're great, Yong."

Yong Ha began to beam. "You stay tomorrow, kid, we make char su ding, wonton soup. You think blood-pressure machine really work?"

"I know it will, Yong. It won't really hurt—just a little to make you stop and think before you lose your temper."

I looked at my watch, got my jacket, apologized for not staying to help with the dishes, told them I'd be back by nine and went out and down to the lobby.

Margaret arrived in the Thunderbird a few minutes later. When I got in beside her, she leaned over and kissed me, then drove over to Riverside Drive, turning north. I felt like a traitor as she chattered on and I stared glumly out the window.

"Is something wrong?" she asked as we neared her home. "You haven't said a word."

"No, of course not, I replied.

"The folks are out at the pool," she said, parking in the driveway. "Your swimsuit is still in the bathhouse from last week. It's lovely this evening, there's a hunter's moon and Daddy has stirred up a pitcher of martinis, one to five, the way you like them."

I needed a martini like I needed two hours of Boch-meir surprises, but I went to the bathhouse and changed to my swimsuit. Margaret had gone inside to change. I walked out of the building to the pool. Oscar and Bertha sat at a table near the pool, their umbrella tilted backward to protect them from a setting sun. They waved and called out greetings as I continued to stand there, half shivering as I thought of entering the water. I dove in suddenly, then swam a lap, coming back to rest at the diving tower. Margaret came out to sit beside her parents in a lounge chair. I felt like a harpooned marlin as the three of them watched their catch admiringly, complimenting themselves, I suspected, on a campaign that had gone off without a hitch.

Oscar was wearing a flowered short-sleeved shirt that flapped over walking shorts, smoking a curved stemmed pipe as he rubbed his huge stomach contentedly. Bertha was wearing a flowered summer dress that seemed two sizes too small, knitting without missing a stitch as she continued to watch me, nodding approvingly. I climbed out of the water and went up the ladder to the high board, standing there looking down, wondering how I could have missed stopping off at the twelve-foot platform. When Oscar removed a glass pitcher of martinis from his ice bucket and waved it at me, I left the board, landing in a belly flop that almost cost me Yong Ha's bok choy and spareribs. I swam slowly toward them to meet the surprise, whatever it might be. As I was climbing out of the pool, the telephone rang beside Oscar's chair. He picked it up, answered, then shook his head, holding the receiver away from him.

"It's for you, Gustav," he said, extending the cord and handing it to me. "Ach, such language!"

I took the phone. "Dr. Golm," I said.

"Little somnobitch gone, Glom! That mother—"

"Now just a minute. Calm down. Tell me slowly what happened."

"He's gone. I go to apartment to get book to study for exam and when I get back—gone. Caught cab downstairs. I—I sorry, Glom. I never think little somnoblitch run away."

"I'll be there as soon as I can."

I put the phone down and turned to Margaret. "You'll have to drive me back at once," I said. "I was keeping my patient until I could deliver him to his mother in the morning, but he's taken off, God only knows where."

"Oh, Gus, he'll be back. Couldn't you stay just a little while. Mamma and Daddy—"

"No, Margaret," Bertha said, resignedly. "With doctor, patient must always come first. You go quick, Gustav. Our surprise will wait. Hurry and change, Margaret."

Oscar was nodding his approval. "You have one martini first, Gustav?"

"No, thank you," I said, then hurried toward the bathhouse and my clothes.

Margaret was waiting in the car when I came out, wearing a cashmere robe. I got in beside her and she backed out, then drove slowly toward Riverside Drive.

"Can't you go a little faster?" I asked, irritably.

She pressed down on the gas and we shot ahead as it remained in passing gear, then braked when we reached the entrance to the drive. When I remained silent, staring away from her toward the river, she began to pout.

"What's wrong with you this evening, Gus? You've hardly said a word to me."

"Forget it," I said. "What was the big surprise?"

"I won't forget it! They think so much of you, want you to like them. We were going to perform for you— Beethoven's 'Archduke' trio. We've been rehearsing for weeks."

"I didn't know your folks were musical."

"It's one of the important things in their lives. Mine, too. They've gone to the Salzburg Festival for the last three years. They're very good. Daddy plays violin with a chamber group that's played at Carnegie Hall, and mother is a fine pianist."

"Do you play?"

"Of course I do. Piano and cello. I'm thinking of taking lessons again on the viola. I thought you liked music."

"I do, for godsake!"

"You don't have to take my head off! You've been rude and angry since I met you this evening. What's wrong?"

"I've got a child I'm responsible for loose in the town and—"

"Its more than that. You were rude on the phone and when I picked you up. It's something else. Tell me what it is."

"Forget it," I said, aware that I'd played it just right. "I've never known you like this."

I stayed silent, pretending anger, ignoring her questions until she had stopped in front of the tower. I opened the door, got out, then faced her through the open window.

"You can give my congratulations to your brilliant Dr. Falstein when he finally gets enough nerve to call you," I said, turning away, but came back when she called to me.

"Gus, tell me this minute what you are trying to insinuate. I hardly know Dr. Falstein, except professionally."

"That's not the way I heard it today. He'll fit right into your family trio."

"Oh Gus, I believe you're jealous. Dr. Falstein means absolutely nothing to me."

"Well, you mean something to him."

I scowled at her, noting her perplexed expression, then ran into the building, not looking back.

It occurred to me as I waited for the elevator that the Bochmeir surprise had served a good purpose. I'd completely forgotten about Falstein's commitment to classical music. He played both flute and viola with a physicians' orchestra that had performed at the A.M.A.'s national meeting and at many local medical affairs. That Oscar and Bertha Bochmeir were so committed to music was a pleasant surprise.

Jimmy, the student who relieves Yong Ha at the desk on his two nights off, stopped me as I passed him.

"Better get up there and calm Yong Ha down, Golm," he said. "I didn't think to stop that patient of yours when he came down and caught a cab. Yong said he'd come down from a state hospital. Want me to call the police? A crazy kid shouldn't be out alone in this town at night."

"Forget it," I said, "and don't say anything to anyone about this boy being crazy. Understand?"

"Sure, Doc. I just wanted to help."

Yong Ha was waiting for me in my apartment, wearing a downcast expression. Before he could explode, I raised my hand.

"Just take it easy," I said, "and let me have the details gently."

"Little somnoblitch just take off, ten minutes after you go."

"Where were you?"

"I got oral exam in morning. I got to get book to study. When I come back, no Stelgis. Jimmy said he take taxi. Sorry, Glom."

"It's all right. He probably knows his way around in this city better than either of us. I guess we'll just have to sit and wait."

"You not call police?"

"Hell no! He'll be back. I'm certain of it."

It was the logical thing to say, and I didn't have much choice. His suitcase and other belongings were in the bedroom. I felt pretty certain he'd return, but I was thinking of what Dr. Karsloff would say to me if he didn't. On a hunch, I decided to call Semminetti and find out if Stelgis had been to see him. He wasn't listed, so I called the medical center operator, identified myself, then asked for Dr. Semminetti's home number, saying it was an emergency. She gave me the number and I dialed it. The phone rang several times. I hung up, turning to Yong Ha.

"You'd better go back to your apartment and study," I said, "and don't blame yourself for what happened. I shouldn't have left him with you. He was my responsibility."

"Sorry, Glom."

"Okay, Yong. Good luck on your exam."

He went out, closing the door softly behind him.

I poured myself a glass of milk, then went into the bedroom, feeling guilty as I opened Steglis' suitcase, even though I knew I was justified. His clothing was neatly folded. I removed one garment at a time, placing them in order on the floor so that I could replace them exactly as they were. There was nothing of interest in the suitcase or the pockets of his clothes. As I started to replace the clothing, I noticed that the lining of the suitcase had been slit at the seam. I slipped my hand into the opening and removed three newspaper clippings.

The first was one of those human-interest items that newspapers use as fillers. It reported a most unusual dinner given by the Adventurer's Club of New York. The *pièce de résistance* was steak from a hairy mastodon, found after a glacial ice slide in Outer Siberia. The mastodon was said to have been dead for an estimated thirty thousand years, but the meat was perfectly preserved and very tasty, similar to beef and venison. The main dish was provided by a member of the club, an anthropologist named Alfred Brodermen, who was an attaché at the American Embassy in Moscow and served as liaison officer between the scientific communities of America and the Soviet Union.

The second clipping, written in the same tongue-in-cheek style, was even more startling, with an Associated Press dateline from Ames, Iowa. It described in some detail thirty-nine prized Jersey calves that had been born—one each year—under extraordinary circumstances. The bull who sired them, it was reported, had been dead two years before any of the calves were born. An Iowa Cattlemen's Association had purchased the bull in Scotland for $38,000 after it had won best of breed in stock throughout Europe. The contract stipulated that the original owners could keep the bull for one year before delivery. However, the new owners had been given a substantial amount of the bull's frozen sperm. This was fortunate, because the bull had contracted an insidious viral disease and died two months after the purchase. The cattlemen, working in co-operation with the local agricultural college, had used a small portion of the sperm to impregnate a valuable Jersey cow in each subsequent year. That the sperm had remained viable after thirty-nine years marked a significant milestone in animal husbandry, proving that great male animals could remain effective for decades after their deaths, perhaps indefinitely.

The third clipping was a recent one from the *Daily News*, which I had read before. Under a headline of "Artificial Insemination Now Common," it reported that many childless couples were now being blessed with children by artificial insemination. Paid donors, usually medical students, were providing sperm. The technique was quite simple and involved spraying the sperm into the mouth of the uterus, a far more effective method of inducing pregnancy than by the hit or miss method of normal copulation.

I knew, as I replaced the clippings, that my patient had not kept them for their human-interest values. I was certain that some of his presumed delusions had their origins in facts. Any child as precocious, well read and imaginative as Stelgis, who was desperately in need of establishing the identity of his father, could take the material I'd discovered and find a logical answer. What would his mother say when I presented her with this conclusion? Only one factor was unrealistic—that his father had been dead thousands of years.

I came out of my own fantasies as I glanced at the clock and saw that it was nine-thirty. He'd been gone more than two hours. If he didn't return within an hour, I would have to call Dr. Karsloff and ask him if I should call the police. If I failed to report the problem and he didn't return, I would be in trouble for the rest of my residency, and could even lose my appointment. Yong Ha and Margaret would support me and I might not have to admit I'd left him with someone else. That a boy of Stelgis' intelligence, and with his history, might slip out while I was in the bathroom would be accepted—although not without criticism—but if it was learned that I had left him with a student to keep a date, Dr. Karsloff would explode and the least I could expect would be a month or two of night duty in the port-mortem lab.

I paced restlessly about the apartment, sipping at a drink, hoping my telephone or door buzzer would sound. When I heard the buzzer a few minutes to ten, I ran to open it, feeling my sense of relief vanish as I looked into Charley Helms' homely face.

"I thought you had a date," I said, continuing to block the half-opened doorway.

"Wasn't my night, I guess. I'd forgotten I'm still on stand-by duty at the emergency room until 7 A.M. They called just after you left. They've been shooting and cutting and burning each other up like crazy tonight, and three acute psychos came in at the same time. What a night! They got a kid from the Bronx DOA about twenty minutes ago. How about a drink?"

"Not tonight, Charley. I'm working on something. What happened to the kid?"

"He was shot in the back of the neck with a dart. Probably from a blowgun, I heard a cop say."

"A dart in the neck shouldn't have killed him, unless it went into the spine."

"This dart, it seems, was coated with curare. They were taking him to Bellevue in a squad car, but when his respiration began to fail, they cut over to us. It went out over the police radio and every reporter in town must have picked it up. Emergency is swarming with them and a television crew arrived just as I was leaving."

"Did you get the boy's name?"

"Nah. They put him in a respirator, but it was too late. Where in the hell would anyone get a curare dart and blowgun, even in this town?"

I knew one place, I thought grimly, feeling my anxiety grow. "You'll have to excuse me, Charley. Good night."

I waited a moment after he had gone, then called the triage desk in the emergency room. Miss Miché answered.

"This is Dr. Golm," I said. "You got a kid DOA, a short time ago, Toby. Do you happen to have his name?"

"Yes, Doctor—Anthony Peroni, Jr. He lived in the upper Bronx, on Carpenter Avenue, just off Gun Hill Road."

"Thank you." I hung up, my worst fears confirmed.

I turned my radio to the twenty-four-hour CBS news station. Its consumer advocate was giving her nightly report on merchant chicanery. I waited impatiently for the news to come on.

Chapter Five

The first bulletins came on at ten and were a rehash of what I'd heard earlier. There was a new hanky-panky going on at City Hall and His Honor had promised a full investigation. . . . Another apartment complex was burning in Flatbush and thought to be another case of arson. . . . Another fare increase was being asked by the commuter railroads. . . . And Billy Carter, in Plains Georgia, had uttered another indiscretion that could only embarrass his brother. . . . "And here is a bulletin just in," the announcer said:

"The body of Anthony Peroni, Jr., a fourteen-year-old Bronx youth, was dead on arrival at the Upper Manhattan University Hospital, killed by a poisoned dart, believed to have been shot from a primitive blowgun. The youth, known to be a member of a street gang that operates in the White Plains Road and Gun Hill Road area of the Bronx, was found unconscious at nine o'clock this evening, under the Gun Hill Bridge, in the park that fronts the Bronx River. The victim was rushed to the emergency room of University Hospital, but was dead from respiratory failure on arrival and could not be resuscitated.

"The father, in his statement to the police, said that his son had received a telephone call at seven forty-five P.M., and that he had left his home immediately, apparently to meet a friend. He said that the boy had just returned from a summer camp in the Catskills, where he had been sent to remove him from what the father described as 'bad neighborhood influences.' It has been learned that Anthony Peroni, Jr., has had three arrests for burglary and assault, and at the time he was placed in the boys' camp was on probation from the Juvenile Court.

"Our reporter, Jimmy Preston, is on stand-by at the Thirty-fourth Precinct Station, and we hope to have a report from him shortly. . . ."

I continued to sit in my chair, feeling shock and anger. My young patient was far from being the innocent, mildly disturbed child I had so easily accepted. He had said that whoever had taken his belongings would pay for it, and that he had known where he lived. The thief had paid; others would pay, too, especially Dr. Gus Golm, in whose care the most obvious murder suspect had been placed. There was only one thing for me to do: call Dr. Karsloff at once and make a clean breast of all that I knew.

I rose from my chair and was starting for the telephone when the CBS announcer interrupted the bulletin he was reading. He repeated a summary of his original report, then said:

"We have our reporter, Jimmy Preston, on the wire live from the Thirty-fourth Precinct station, in Washington Heights. What do you have to report, Jimmy? Come on in.

" 'I have just talked with Lieutenant of Detectives John MacMann, who has been assigned to the case. The cause of death has been officially confirmed by pathologists at University Hospital as acute respiratory failure, due to curare-induced paralysis of the respiratory muscular system.'

"Do they have any idea at all of where the dart might have come from?

" 'Not officially, but it is now assumed that it came from the American Museum of Natural History. Lieutenant MacMann was able to contact a curator at the museum, Dr. Harrison Berger, an anthropologist who is an expert on South American jungle tribes. From a description of the dart, given him by phone, he tentatively identified it as similar to three darts that were stolen from a display case in the museum's Hall of Man section in July of last year. The glass case had been broken and the darts and a blowgun were taken. Dr. Berger, however, was emphatic in saying that the darts had been deactivated of all poisonous substances before going on display. He—excuse me just a moment. What is it, Lieutenant? Thank you—thank you very much. Lieutenant MacMann has just been informed that the dead boy, Anthony Peroni, Jr., was one of three youths arrested at the museum in August last year, when caught with antique coins taken from a collection on display there. The lieutenant has also confirmed that Peroni's street gang recently split into two groups and that there has been a great deal of violence between the two factions. He suspects that Peroni's death is a result of internecine war between the two gangs. I guess that's all I have at present.'

"Thank you, Jimmy, and keep us informed. . . ."

I remained seated in my chair for several minutes, wanting to believe the police assumption that this death was just another in New York's gang wars, but my intuition told me something else. Neither the curator nor the museum would ever permit poisonous darts to go on public display. A mistake was possible, of course, but someone who had free run of the museum shouldn't find it difficult to obtain the curare, even though it might be locked away. And my patient had asked specifically to go home and pick up something he needed.

Resigned to my fate, I went to the telephone and started to dial Dr. Karsloff's number, but the door buzzer sounded before I could complete it. I dropped the phone and ran to open the door. Stelgis Kara-Kash stood there, minus the jacket he had worn when he left. His forehead was covered with encrusted blood from a deep abrasion. His shirt and trousers were splattered with what looked like half-dried mud, and his eyes were glistening with tears as his lips trembled.

"Oh, Gus," he cried, lunging toward me to place his arms around my midriff, burying his face in my stomach. He was trembling violently.

I maneuvered him inside and to the sofa, forcing him to lie down, then ran for my medical bag.

He began to sob, protesting, as I cleansed the abrasion with alcohol. "How did you get this?" I demanded. "And all that mud on your clothes?" When he didn't respond, I shook him and repeated my questions.

He sniffled for a moment, then said, "I fell."

"Where?"

"Under the bridge. I was running and there was soft mud. . . . Oh, Gus, I'm—I'm—"

"Just lie quietly," I said sternly. "When did you have your last tetanus booster shot?"

"At camp. They gave all of us shots. Oh, Gus, I'm afraid." He began to shake and tremble again.

"Just lie quietly until I finish this. There's nothing to be afraid of here." When he continued to sob and shake, I removed a capsule from my bag, went for a glass of water, then came back to him. "Here, take this."

"What is it?"

"Just a mild tranquilizer. Swallow it."

He obeyed meekly, then looked up at me with anguished eyes, imploring me to not be angry with him. I went to his suitcase and removed his pajamas, bringing them to him. I helped him undress and get into the pajamas, then went to the kitchen and got him a glass of milk and some cookies.

"I—I can't eat, Gus. Really—"

"Go ahead and drink the milk, then you are going to answer some questions. Understand? I want no lies, no evasions. You are in serious trouble this time, Stelgis, and we'll have no nonsense."

"Can't we wait until morning? I don't want to—"

"Now! Finish your milk."

I continued to watch him, aware that he was coming out of a severe traumatic experience, knowing that I should question him before he came out of shock and regained control of his emotions. The telephone rang and we both jumped noticeably. It was Dr. Semminetti.

"Golm, I've just come home and found out that you brought Stelgis here this afternoon. Can you tell me why?"

"Yes. He wanted to pick up something from his mother's

apartment. She's not getting in until tomorrow morning and he's staying with me tonight."

"I know that. Did you accompany him into the building?"

"No. I stayed in the car, in a restricted zone. The doorman went with him."

"I see. Thank you very much, Dr. Golm."

"Why are you so concerned, Doctor?"

"I was only curious about why you would bring him here. Good night."

Steglis would not meet my eyes when I returned. "That was your old friend Dr. Semminetti," I said, pulling a chair forward so that I could sit beside him. "He wanted to know why I permitted you to enter his apartment this afternoon," I lied, watching his face closely.

He grimaced, continuing to lie with his eyes closed.

"Why did you go to his apartment, Stelgis?"

He waited several seconds, took a deep breath, then seemed to relax, and I knew that the drug was taking effect.

"I went to get something."

"What? I want the truth, Stelgis."

"Some money."

"That doesn't make sense. You had a twenty-dollar bill and change for another twenty when you paid our check at McDonald's this afternoon. I saw—"

"I needed more than that. Oh, Gus, he doesn't mind. She always pays him back. He always keeps a hundred dollars in cash on hand, mostly for us. She's always forgetting to cash a check for weekends."

"How much money did you need?"

"Fifty dollars."

"What for?"

"I was going to give it to him."

"Who?"

"You know—Tony Peroni, the kid who stole my things at camp."

"Stelgis, you haven't seen that boy since they took you to the hospital."

"I called him when I was in the apartment. That's why I wanted you to take me there. He said I could have my stuff back for fifty dollars."

"And you called him at his home again this evening, around eight, didn't you?"

"No, Gus. I didn't. I told him this afternoon that I'd meet him with the money between eight and nine, if I could get away from you."

"Where?"

"In the park by the river, under the Gun Hill Road bridge."

"What was so important about those papers he took? The truth, Stelgis."

"They belonged to Uncle Ted."

"How did you come by them?"

He hesitated, opened his eyes, met my gaze, colored and said, "We had an overnight camp-out, up in the mountains. I slipped away and went to town and caught the bus."

"That was on Saturday and you were in Uncle Ted's apartment early Sunday morning."

"How did you know?"

"He told me. You apparently got back to camp without being missed."

He grinned for the first time since coming home. "I told them I got lost in the woods."

"You're a devious little rascal," I said, "but you'd better not be devious with me. Was there anything in those papers to connect them with Uncle Ted?"

"Sure. It was a folder, the kind he used for his case histories. His name and address is on all of them."

"What were the papers about?"

"I don't really know, except they were about me."

"Cut the bull, Stelgis."

"Honest, I don't know, Gus. He writes his case histories in Italian, so that no one else can read them."

"Why did you keep them then?"

"I was going to Xerox them at the museum, but the business office was locked on Sunday. I took the stuff with me and was going to copy them at the library in Hanover, then bring them back before he got home from California."

"Why did you want to copy them?"

"I was going to get an Italian dictionary and find out what he'd written about me."

"Why are you so sure it was about you?"

"He had it filed under the 'K's, and it was the only thing there. He used to take my anthropometric measurements when I was little."

Another part of the jigsaw puzzle fell into place to explain the Stelgis's fantasies, and in spite of my fears for his future I could feel only pity for him.

"All right, Stelgis, this is the big one—why did you kill Tony Peroni?"

His eyes widened and he looked at me in amazement. "I haven't seen him since I left camp. Honest, Gus! He didn't show up tonight like he promised."

His reaction couldn't have been faked. I knew instinctively as I watched him that he had told the truth.

"What happened then, if you didn't meet him?"

"I waited a long time, then went back to the cab, but it was gone. I gave him twenty dollars and he promised to wait for me on Gun Hill Road, but he just kept my money and—"

"What time was that?"

"A little after nine."

"Where have you been for the past two hours?"

"I—I had to walk back. Gus."

"You had fifty dollars and—"

"They took it away from me. I tried to run back into the park, but I fell and they caught me under the bridge."

"Who caught you?"

"A gang of boys. They took my money and watch, then ran. I tried to slip into the subway, but the guard caught me. When I got outside, I ran away and walked back here. I got lost twice and—and—" The rest was lost in sobs. He finally managed to ask how I knew Tony Peroni was dead.

"It's been on the radio. Do you want to know how he was killed?"

He turned away from me and began to sob convulsively.

I went to the kitchen and mixed myself another scotch and soda, feeling a desperate need for it. When I returned he was sleeping soundly. I picked him up and took him into the bedroom, putting him under the cover. Then, facing up to the inevitable, I went to the telephone and dialed Dr. Karsloff's home number. He was still up and answered immediately. Something in my voice must have alerted him to my state of mind, because he listened with only minimal interruptions as I gave him an honest summary of the situation, omitting only that I hadn't been there when my patient had slipped away. Fortunately, he had heard the news report of the Peroni boy's murder, and when I suggested that we probably should inform the police of Stelgis's presence in the vicinity of the murder, he was against it.

"Don't feel too upset about this, Golm. Another report just came in before you called. The police have apparently got the case solved. That rival gang had threatened to kill the Peroni kid—that's why his old man sent him to camp. They've taken several members into custody. Our patient is disturbed enough without our putting him through another ordeal with the police. Have him in my office by nine with your recommendations ready to present to his mother. I'll back you on them. And, oh yes, Golm, what do you intend to do about that road tar that's messed up the underside of my Mercedes's fenders?"

"Maybe I can run it down to that do-it-yourself car-wash place on Broadway. They have a steam hose, and I have the day off."

"That's an excellent idea, Golm. Good night."

I felt my anxiety pass, but took a Nembutal, just to make certain I got some sleep.

Chapter Six

I woke shortly after seven Tuesday morning, feeling a cramp in my neck from sleeping on the sofa, but totally recovered from two fatiguing days and lost sleep. I went to the bedroom door, opening it quietly. My guest was snoring with a steady rhythm.

I put on a pot of coffee and turned the radio on softly, but there were no new reports on the Peroni boy's death. I carried my first cup of coffee to the living room and was drinking it when Steglis came out of the bedroom, fully dressed.

"Are you hungry?" I asked.

"Yeah. Can I make breakfast? Sophia lets me do it all the time."

"Go ahead."

Bacon, eggs and toast were soon on the counter, and he poured me a fresh cup of coffee. The radio was still on CBS, and a rehash of last night's report was being given by a new announcer. We both listened, but avoided each other's eyes. When he moved on to a new bulletin, Steglis met my eyes.

"I think I hated Tony Peroni, Gus," he said, "but I couldn't kill him."

"The social service worker at Hanover said you tried to drown him at camp."

"That's not true. I knew what I was doing. I would have pulled him out, if the others hadn't—"

"I'm sure you would have," I said. "Would you mind telling me about those trips Joe said you used to take down to Broadway—those porno photographs you used to bring home?"

He blushed, almost choked on his toast, then looked away from me. "Joe talks too much," he said. "I—I don't go for that stuff, but the boys in my class back in Chicago do. I guess I was trying to be a big shot. You won't tell her, will you?"

"Of course not," I said, smiling. "Once when I was about your age I was on the midway at our county fair and slipped under the tent to watch a naked woman dance. They wouldn't sell tickets to anyone under twenty-one."

"Did anything happen to you because—"

"I saw my father and the president of our bank there, so I slipped back out before they could see me."

"Would he have whipped you again, if he'd caught you?"

"I don't think so. I think he might have asked me not to tell mother that I'd found him there."

He laughed suddenly. "Is your father really angry because you went into psychiatry?"

"I don't think so, not any more. He wanted me to come back home and take over his general practice. I think he realizes now that each of us has to do his own thing."

"Is he nice—your father?"

"Very nice, and I love him very much, now that we've become friends."

"Weren't you always friends?"

"I doubt that any boy can be friends with his father until he finds out who he is. Tell me about Sophia."

"You'll like her, Gus, I know you will. We have good times together. I wouldn't do anything to hurt Sophia. She gets so lonely at times, and cries a lot, and Uncle Ted is always coming around to upset her."

"How?"

"Oh, you know how he is, always coming at the wrong time. They argue about me a lot."

"Do you think he might be in love with her?"

"Uncle Ted! Never. Once, though, I heard him say something they didn't mean me to hear."

"Do you do a lot of eavesdropping when he's around?"

"Sure. I learn a lot listening to them."

"About what?"

"Oh, Grandfather, the way things used to be."

"You said he used to take your anthropometric measurements. Why would he do that?"

"He wanted to be an anthropologist. Grandfather wouldn't talk to him for a long time, not after he switched to medicine and psychiatry."

"How old is Sophia, Stelgis?"

"Thirty-two. She doesn't look that old, especially when she's asleep."

"Do you watch her when she's asleep?"

"Sometimes. She usually catches me at it."

"And what happens then?"

"We usually have a wrestling match. Did you ever tell your mother that you saw your dad in that girlie show?"

"Of course not. It's quite normal that men, and boys, should want to see girlie shows. Have you got any girl friends in Chicago?"

He blushed, thought a moment, then said, "One, I guess—Shirley. It's always between her and me who gets the top rating in our class. Her father is a physicist."

"Do you ever have her over to your apartment?"

"Nah, Sophia doesn't like her, not since we skipped class and went down to the Field Museum alone. But Shirley's nice."

"I'm sure she is. Do you want to tell me now why you went into that meat locker and took your temperature for eight hours, every thirty minutes?"

He blushed again, avoiding my eyes. "I've read a lot about hypothermia," he said. "One of the neurosurgeons used to cool his patients down to almost freezing before he clipped their aneurysms. I only lost a degree of temperature in that cold room over nine hours."

"But hypothermia isn't used anymore. They used to do it quickly to retard the heartbeat and hemorrhage. When you do it as you did, the body's metabolism goes to work and raises body heat to counteract the cold. Your reaction to that meat room was about normal. You lost less than a degree of temperature, and it's often that low under normal circumstances at night."

He appeared to be disappointed. "Want some more coffee, Gus?" he asked, changing the subject.

I nodded and he poured. I stopped him when the cup was half full.

"You told me last night, Stelgis, that you picked up fifty dollars from Dr. Semminetti's apartment. Does he leave that kind of cash just lying around?"

"He keeps it in a medical dictionary on his desk."

"Something else has been bothering me." I met his eyes, waited a moment, then said, "I believe Tony Peroni delivered your papers to Dr. Semminetti yesterday. Did you look in his files again when you were in his apartment?"

He appeared surprised. "How do you know that he brought them back?"

"Some boy whose description fitted Tony brought an envelope to him. Joe took him to Dr. Semminetti's apartment. He didn't have the envelope when he came out, but he had money. One thing bothers me. Dr. Semminetti's home number is unlisted. How did Tony know how to reach him?"

"His Centrex number at the Medical Center was on his folder. He could have called him there."

"Yes, that probably explains it. What are you going to tell Uncle Ted when he asks you about taking a case history from his files?"

"He won't ask. He's caught me trying to read his case histories before."

"Have you ever tried to talk to him about—about who your father might be?"

"Lot's of times. Sophia too. They just say that he was a very nice man and never knew that I was born."

"I guess that makes a person wonder sometimes."

"It's after eight," he said, changing the subject, again. "Aren't we supposed to meet her at nine?"

"Yes, we'd better get ready to go. How did you lose your jacket?"

"One of the boys came back and took that too. I have another one in my camp locker. I'll get it."

I went into my bathroom, shaved, showered, then went

into the bedroom and dressed, leaving Stelgis watching the tube. When I came out a few minutes later, he had disappeared. I ran into the hall and to the elevator. The left one was above me, coming down; the right one was moving rapidly toward ground level. I pressed the button, waiting for the left elevator to reach my floor. When it stopped, I got in and pressed the lobby button. There was nobody in the lobby, but the day clerk was at the desk. He said that only one resident had used the elevator during the past few minutes. I went into the stairwell and walked up five floors, until I was out of breath, stopping to listen for steps, but there was no sound. I finally took the elevator to my floor and hurried into my empty apartment, condemning myself for letting him disappear. On a hunch, I went outside and down to Yong Ha's room. I knocked. Stelgis opened it, smiling. "Ready to go, Gus?" he asked. "I came down to tell Yong Ha good-bye, in case I don't get to see him again."

"You want some fresh coffee, Glom?" Yong Ha asked. "Maybe we get prosthesis made up this week? I think about what you say. Stelgis say he come back and help me learn to use it. Okay?"

"Okay. I'll talk to the instrument shop about it today. We'd better be on our way, Stelgis. Don't screw up on your oral exam, Yong. They know your weakness and may try to trigger your temper. Just keep remembering that, then think before your speak."

"Okay, Glom."

We left the tower at a quarter of nine and walked down to the institute. Dr. Falstein was parking his car when we neared the front entrance. He waved to me. We waited until he had locked his door. He smiled as he joined us.

"Morning, Golm," he said. "I'm sorry we missed our session yesterday. Dr. Karsloff explained why. Perhaps we can work it in late this afternoon. I'll be away tomorrow. Suppose we make it at three o'clock."

"But I have the day off and things to do. Couldn't—"

"See you at three, Golm. I must run now. I'm afraid I've kept Dr. Helms waiting."

I swore softly as I watched him enter the building and run toward an elevator. I hoped that Charley Helms, made to wait, would be angry enough to put some imagination into the charade I'd asked him to perform.

I stopped in the lobby to study the duty roster, pleased to see that I'd been taken off the emergency service and would start on receiving on Wednesday.

We caught the express elevator, getting off at the penthouse, where the director had his suite of offices. Miss Thomas smiled at us. "Good morning, Dr. Golm, and this must be Stelgis," she said. "Your mother just called from the airport and is on her way here now. I think you should wait here with me while Dr. Golm talks with Dr. Karsloff. Go right in, Dr. Golm, he is expecting you."

I watched Stelgis settle into the plush sofa and pick up the morning *Times* from the coffee table. I winked at him, then went through the door, my anxiety mounting as usual.

Dr. Karsloff was writing on a scratch pad. He glanced up for a moment, nodded toward a chair in front of him, then continued to ignore me. My anxiety grew as I waited, watching him scratch viciously with his pen.

"Well, how's your patient this morning?" he asked.

"Fine. I've had a good talk with him, and learned quite a bit. These fantasies that caused so much concern to the Hanover staff seem to have at least a foundation in facts, if you place yourself in the boy's position."

"Bring me up to date before Sophia gets here. Donaldson just gave me a summary by phone. He doesn't believe the kid needs hospitalization."

I gave him a brief report of all I'd learned about Stelgis, trying not to reveal any of my own feelings.

"It's fantastic," he said. "I've read about and been involved with similar cases, but none as bizarre as this one. You said yesterday you thought it might be good to separate the kid from his mother for a while. I doubt that she'll go for it, but you can suggest it. Why do you think they should be separated?"

"I believe Stelgis is just beginning to become sexually curious. I know he goes to those peep-show machines in Broadway arcades, and that he's brought back postcards. He said he likes to watch his mother sleep, but that she always wakes up to catch him at it, and they wrestle. I suspect that their relationship is more like brother and sister than mother and child."

"Yes, that's quite likely. She's always been a strange one, totally dominated by that angry old man, her father. I doubt she's ever had a normal relationship with any man. Semminetti hasn't helped the situation any, fretting like an old mother hen, trying to direct her life."

"Do you think he might be in love with her?"

"Who knows about Seminnetti? But he was the only one she had to turn to after the old man died. She had a serious breakdown the year before this boy was born."

"Was she delivered at this medical center?"

"Yes, old Dr. Snyder had the case. He was chairman of the department and chief of the Obs-Gyn service and one of her father's few close friends. God, he must be well past eighty now. Stayed on as professor emeritus for a few years after retirement, dabbling in research at the Institute for Human Reproduction. Still lives over in Englewood, I believe."

"Do you think he might talk with me?"

"Maybe, if you could justify it as related to helping your patient. Snyder is old, but he's still alert—or was when I last talked to him at the center's fiftieth anniversary celebrations. I believe he and Semminetti still keep in touch."

"You know Dr. Kara-Kash, Dr. Karsloff. Perhaps if you made recommendations, she would more likely accept them than if—"

"Golm, it's your case. I believe you have a major problem ahead of you; I'll be most interested to see how you handle it."

"Yes, sir. What nationality was Dr. Kara-Kash? It's an unusual name and—"

"All I know is what he once told a reporter. He said he was part Greek, part Turk and part Mongol and that he'd inherited the best genes of each race."

"One more question. If Dr. Kara-Kash has never been interested in men, how could she have become pregnant?"

"That's a question a lot of us have been asking for the last twelve years. When do you plan to clean up my car?"

"Maybe when we get through with our meeting. I have to see Dr. Falstein at three. I was supposed to see him yesterday, but—"

"I know, you volunteered to go to Hanover, and it was

71

damned noble of you. How about keeping the boy at the institute for a few days of observation and a complete work-up, if Sophia approves?"

"I wouldn't want to have him hospitalized at this time, but we might see him as an outpatient."

"Good. Where the hell is she? I've got a meeting at—"

His intercom crackled and Miss Thomas announced Dr. Kara-Kash's arrival. I followed Dr. Karsloff out to his waiting room. She was sitting on the edge of the sofa, facing her son. The boy was smiling, obviously happy to see her.

"Hello, Sophia."

She was startled by Dr. Karsloff's voice and rose quickly from the sofa, turning to face him. "Good morning, Dr. Karsloff."

When the director turned aside to introduce her to me, I looked into her face for the first time. I felt my pulse quicken and for a moment couldn't speak. All of the pictures I'd formed in my mind were blotted out. I stammered something, unable to turn my eyes away from her. She was the most beautiful, most feminine woman I had ever seen, even though her lovely eyes were tired and circled from lack of sleep. Her black curly hair, cut short, made her look like a young girl. Her eyes were deep violet, dimples formed at the corners of her mouth and her thin, straight nose and rather long neck were all enhanced by an even suntan.

"I repeat, Dr. Golm. This is Dr. Sophia Kara-Kash."

I came out of shock, glanced at Dr. Karsloff, who was grinning, then stepped forward, offering my hand as I said, "I—I'm very glad to meet Stelgis's mother. I have—"
She barely touched my fingers, then withdrew her hand.

"Sorry to have to run to a meeting, Sophia. Will you please go on into my office? Dr. Golm will join you in a minute. You stay out here with Miss Thomas, Stelgis. Could I speak to you outside for a moment, Golm?"

I followed him out to the elevator. He was wearing the same grin when he turned to face me. "I've been waiting a long time to see it, Golm, and it was worth it. Face like a pickled quince, I believe you suggested. Looks like Elizabeth Taylor must have looked twenty years ago, doesn't she? Well, don't get your hopes too high. You're the institute's leading stallion, but I'm still betting on the mare in the short race. My keys are at the desk downstairs. Have a nice day."

He was leering at me as the elevator door closed in front of him. I returned to the waiting room, where Stelgis came forward to greet me. "She likes you, Gus," he said. "I know she does. I can always tell."

I walked past him into the inner office. She was standing at the window, looking down on the Hudson's wrinkled surface where a barge, towed by a tugboat a fraction of its size, plowed a white furrow toward the bridge, circled by one curious gull. She jumped when I spoke, turning quickly to face me, tears gleaming in her eyes.

"Won't you sit down, please, Dr. Kara-Kash," I said. "I know you must be exhausted, but this won't take long."

She hesitated, avoided my eyes, then started to sit down, but turned and remained standing. Her fingers were trembling as she twisted a handkerchief in her hand.

"I want to thank you for being so kind to Stelgis," she said. "I only had a moment with him, but he adores you. Dr. Semminetti met me at customs and told me the details. Could—do you think we might postpone this meeting until this evening? I'm really exhausted and—and I'd like a little more time with Stelgis. Perhaps we could meet for dinner."

"Of course," I replied. "There's no rush at all. And you mustn't be too concerned about Stelgis. He's a fine boy and—and he's going to be all right. I'll meet you wherever you might suggest."

"Could we meet at seven at the House of Chan? It's on Seventh Avenue, at Fifty-first Street, I believe."

"It's a fine restaurant. I know it well. At seven."

She returned to the window for a moment. "It's so beautiful, the river and the green palisades. I used to watch it with my father from the college's research building. I've missed it." She turned to me. "Thank you, Dr. Golm, for being so understanding."

I remained seated, watching her walk gracefully from the room. When I regained my senses and rushed out to say good-bye to Stelgis they were entering the elevator. Stelgis grinned and waved at me as the door closed.

I went down to the lobby to pick up Dr. Karsloff's keys,

then drove down to the car wash on Broadway. The asphalt hadn't yet set on the fenders and came off easily. I put the car through the automatic washer, then wiped it down and drove it back to the institute.

When I reached my apartment at ten-thirty, I called Charley Helms at his station on the twelfth floor.

"How did it go with our friend this morning?" I asked.

"He was in something of a daze when I left."

"I hope you didn't spread it too thick."

"Well, maybe just a bit. I said you and Margaret had just quarreled over him. He thinks Margaret has his picture and that item that appeared about him and his musical accomplishments in our newspaper. It made him think, buddy, believe me it did. He even let me out after only twenty minutes. I've also had a little chat with Margaret."

"How did she react?"

"Like any woman who learns she has a secret admirer. You must have set the stage for me. She knew I came on duty from my session with Falstein, and wanted to know, in an indirect way of course, if he had ever mentioned her. I said he was always asking questions about her. She was hardly with it when she helped me cut down a vessel for a transfusion. Oh, my God, you're not going to believe it—"

"Whatha hell's wrong?"

"Here comes our therapist, in a fresh white coat, his beard trimmed, walking on his toes with his shoulders back. He always makes his rounds in the afternoon—he hasn't been on this floor mornings as long as I've worked it. See you, pal."

I made myself a sandwich, downed it with a glass of milk, set my alarm for two-thirty, then flopped down on my sofa. I was thinking of Sophia Kara-Kash's lovely eyes when I suddenly remembered my promise to Yong Ha. I called Jensen at the instrument shop, explained in detail what I needed and told him it was for a special research project, but that I'd pay for any materials he didn't have. He said there was no problem, he'd try to have it for me by the end of the week.

I returned to my fantasies and was asleep in a few minutes.

Chapter Seven

I woke shortly after two before the alarm went off, and turned on my radio. A summary of the Peroni boy's murder was given along with an update. The boys who had been taken into custody following the killing had been released for lack of evidence, but the police were still investigating. The dart had been officially confirmed as one taken from the museum, but the curator remained positive that the stolen darts had been free of any poisonous substance.

I felt relaxed and up to the challenge as I returned to the institute and went up to the fifth floor, where Dr. Falstein has his office.

"You can go right in, Dr. Golm, he's waiting for you," the secretary said.

I entered Falstein's small, cozy office, furnished like a living room. He poured our coffee as I sat down in my usual place on the sofa, then leaned back in his big chair, studying me, waiting for me to open the conversation. I noted his immaculate white coat and his neat beard, but refused to meet his eyes. When I continued to be glum, he opened the session as usual.

"Do you have any problems with patients that you'd like to discuss with me?"

"No."

"I understand from Dr. Karsloff that you've been assigned to a most unusual case."

"They're all unusual, aren't they?"

"My, my, but we're in a sour mood today. What would you like to talk about?"

"If you want the truth, I'd like to forget this and future sessions. If I needed psychotherapy, which I don't, I'd prefer to choose my own therapist."

"Of course you would. I seriously doubt that the progress we've made to date has been worth the loss of your time and mine. Last week, I believe, we were discussing your relationship with your mother. You said—"

"Forget my mother. We had a normal, loving relationship. She stood up for me against my father and grandfather when I rebelled against following them to medical school. It was only a diversionary tactic. It was mother, really, who talked me into realizing their ambitions for me."

"But you wasted a year, I believe, after finishing college."

"What do you mean, 'wasted'? I got a job in Chicago and had a good time after four years of drudgery. I probably made a big mistake by giving in to them."

"Would you like to amplify that statement?"

"What I'd like to amplify is something quite different. Why don't you let me ask you a question for a change?"

"Of course. What in particular is bothering you, Dr. Golm?"

"I want to know why you're so interested in my relationship with Miss Bochmeir. You never miss an opportunity to drag her into our conversation."

He looked away from me, thought for a moment, then said, "I wasn't aware that I'd displayed any more interest in your relationship with Miss Bochmeir than in other women we've discussed."

"Oh, no? My bitch is this, Dr. Falstein—my social life is my own business. I don't think it abnormal for a twenty-nine-year-old man to be attracted to women. The average American male is married by the time he's through college. But not doctors. They're too damned concerned with their careers. They used to marry nurses to support them while doing their internships and resident training, then divorced them when they had no further use for them. When they started paying us decent salaries during training, such marriages became rare. We pay our own way, find normal outlets for our sexual drives—at least most of us do. I assure you that I am quite normal."

"My dear Golm. I have never had a serious doubt about your normalcy. These sessions are not required to provide serious therapy. We hope to help you learn to handle your own emotions when dealing with patients, to help you gain insights into specific weaknesses so that you can deal with them. When our alumni leave this institution, its reputation goes with them. One thing in your relationship with women does concern me."

"May I ask what?"

"You never form lasting attachments. Your reputation hasn't gone unnoticed by other members of our faculty. It seems likely to some of them that you may be incapable of forming a lasting relationship with any woman, if you haven't done so at your age."

"Well, that's pretty goddamned stupid, coming from you! I was a damned fool for not settling on neurology, as I wanted to. I wouldn't be—"

"Just a moment, Golm. What are you trying to imply?"

"When I finally find a beautiful woman I care enough about to marry, I find one of our esteemed professors moving in on me."

"Tell me exactly what you mean by that, Golm."

"All right, dammit, I'll tell you. Why does my fiancée, just when we've gotten to the point of talking of marriage, start singing your praises to me? Especially since you began giving concerts at national medical meetings. All I hear is how wonderful it is for a physician to love music, when she knows I couldn't hum 'Dixie' if my life depended on it."

He sat up in his chair, startled by my show of anger, then remembered his role and relaxed, forcing a smile. "I haven't the slightest idea what you're talking about."

"You and your damned viola and piccolo—that's all I hear—"

"I do *not* play the piccolo, Golm!"

"Well, flute or whatever it is."

"Just a moment, Golm. It's pleasant to hear that one is admired and respected, but—"

"And her family is worse than she is, always blaming me because I never learned to play a musical instrument."

"I wasn't aware that—"

"Music is that family's most important thing in life. The old man has a multi-million-dollar business, one of the finest estates in Riverdale, but he's prouder of having played with his chamber group in Carnegie Hall. Bertha is almost as bad—she's an accomplished pianist and organist. Margaret plays the cello. You and your viola are all they need for a family chamber group. I'm beginning to fit in like a one-legged man at an ass-kicking contest, Dr. Falstein, and I don't like it. I don't like it at all!"

"Just relax, Golm, and let's explore this hostility toward me."

"Good afternoon, Doctor. I've had it for today."

He didn't try to call me back as I ran out of his office, but sat there with a stunned expression.

I got back to my apartment shortly after four. Yong Ha's door opened when I came out of the elevator.

"How'd the exam go this morning, Yong? Did you keep yourself under control?"

"Vandermleer, that somnoblitchin mother—all the time interrupt, all the time yell. I in trouble, Golm. We get prosthesis soon, maybe?"

"We'll have it by Friday."

"Stelgis come with mother to get his things. I let them in your apartment. You not mind, Glom?"

"No, of course not. How was he?"

"Got very beautiful mamma, Glom. Nice woman. You want me cook dinner?"

"No, I've got a dinner date downtown. But there *is* something you can do for me since you don't have to work tonight."

"Okay, Glom."

"Would you go to the library and run through the indexes for publications by a Professor Brodermen? He is, or was, a professor of anthropology at the University of Pennsylvania. The first name might be Alfred. Don't go into the journals, but just give me a bibliography, if you find anything. You might do the same for Dr.

Sophia Kara-Kash. You know what I need, like you did for me on endocrine disorders for my last paper."

"Okay. I leave it on your desk."

I returned to my apartment, took a bath, then laid out my new suit. I debated between two ties, choosing the more conservative one. I mixed myself a very dry martini and sat down to watch the early news. There was no mention of the Peroni boy's murder, which had been pre-empted by three new murders.

I dressed just before five and went over to the independent subway line. As I clung to my strap, feeling the rush hour crush on all sides, I thought again that if our farm animals in Indiana had been this abused, the SPCA would have been out to protest immediately. I was suddenly glad that I had left early, giving me time for an extra martini before Dr. Kara-Kash arrived. I was still feeling residuals of shock, aware that something important had happened in my life. I felt certain that she was undeveloped in many areas and that her rapidly maturing son had become a surrogate for the male companionship she needed, but I also felt there was nothing unwholesome in their relationship.

It occurred to me as I entered the restaurant that Dr. Semminetti would have talked to her by now and that I'd have to overcome the negative picture he had undoubtedly painted of my character.

It was still early for the dinner crowd and the restaurant was nearly empty. I checked with the hostess at the door to see if she had made a reservation. She checked the book and she had. I asked to be called when she arrived and walked into the bar, where two or three men were working up courage to make the nightly trip home. I took a stool at the far end and ordered a dry martini on the rocks. I stirred it, anticipating the first cold, astringent sip. As I raised the glass, still thinking of the problems that I would soon have to face, I felt someone come from behind me and take the chair alongside. I heard a familiar sniffing and knew before I turned that it would be Dr. Semminetti. He smiled at me, his hostility apparently gone.

"Good evening, Dr. Semminetti. What brings you to this part of town?"

"I share an office on Park Avenue, and have evening appointments on Tuesdays, Thursdays and Fridays. I occasionally stop here for dinner on my way to the office."

"Will you have a drink with me?"

"Thank you, Golm."

He ordered a glass of French wine, specified the type of glass in which it was to be served, asking that it be at room temperature. He asked to see the bottle before it was poured. I watched the impassive face of the Chinese bartender. Only his eyes betrayed his disapproval, but he followed instructions, pouring a small amount of wine into the glass, waiting for Dr. Semminetti to taste it before he finished filling the glass.

I watched, fascinated, as he rolled the wine around in his mouth, eyes closed, expecting him to be disappointed, but he smiled instead, nodded approvingly to the waiter, then turned to me. "I was hoping that I might find you here, Golm," he said, glancing at his watch. "Sophia is always a little late. If I was short with you yesterday, I hope you'll understand that I had good reason to be upset."

"I realized that, Doctor."

He put the glass down and began to stroke his mustache.

He hesitated, then said, "I don't know what you and Dr. Karsloff have in mind for Stelgis, but I'm asking you to withdraw from the case as soon as you can. I intend to discuss this with him when he can find time to see me alone. You'll need to see Dr. Kara-Kash, of course, but I do not wish you to continue with this child. He has problems far beyond your experience. The same is true of his mother."

"You mean professionally, sir?"

He frowned, and his piercing, cold blue eyes seemed to bore into mine. "Professionally and otherwise."

"Could you please explain what you mean by 'otherwise'?"

"Your social activities at the medical center have not completely escaped me, Dr. Golm. Sophia is a beautiful woman, but she is also very vulnerable, on the edge of serious emotional illness. I will not permit her to be—"

"Just one moment, sir. If you are trying to imply that I have interests in Dr. Kara-Kash other than—"

"Please don't interrupt me, Golm. I don't believe you fully understand my motives for taking you into my confidence. Sophia's mother, as you probably do not know, died in a catatonic stupor—Sophia has a genetic heritage that cannot be ignored. I will not permit anyone—you, Leon Karsloff, her son—to upset a balance that is precarious at best. She is a brilliant, dedicated scientist. I know her weaknesses and her strengths better than anyone. She has survived one brutally traumatic experience, but I doubt that she can survive another."

I felt my anger rising as I watched his smug face. "Dr. Kara-Kash did not strike me as a borderline psychopathic personality, not even a potential—"

"You are a two-year resident in psychiatry, Golm, and you are to withdraw from this case at the earliest possible moment. Do I make myself completely clear?"

"Are you threatening me, sir? I didn't volunteer to handle this case; I was assigned to it by the director of service. I've become fond of Stelgis, who does need help, perhaps desperately."

He sniffed, took another drink of wine, then said, "I'll explain to Leon. You can't possibly help, but you can do irreparable harm."

"I simply don't understand you, Dr. Semminetti."

"For reasons that you should understand now, I was less than frank with the Hanover staff yesterday. Stelgis is not psychotic, but he has a very serious character disorder, which has nothing whatever to do with intelligence. He cannot be compared with any case you have known or read about. We've had serious problems with him and they become more serious as he matures."

"What kind of problems, sir?"

"I do not believe that Stelgis can experience normal emotions. I doubt that he can experience fear, anger, as we understand it, or real love. The facade is there, he knows what is expected of him, but he responds in his own primitive way to emotional stimuli—he's capable of—"

"I just can't accept that, sir. He seems like a warm, affectionate little boy who needs understanding."

"You *must* accept it, Golm." He smiled in that arrogant manner that infuriates his students and colleagues. He remained silent, studying his wine, waiting for me to speak, but I decided to wait him out. "I am presuming that you and Dr. Karsloff have recommendations to make to Sophia?"

"Nothing definite, sir. We both feel that he could benefit from boarding school, perhaps one that specializes in helping disturbed adolescents."

His eyebrows lifted imperceptibly. "That's an excellent suggestion. I've been talking with Sophia along the same lines. Actually, she had intended to have him accompany her on her trip to Paris, but I convinced her that he might benefit from camp life. He has reached a stage when—"

"When he is becoming sexually curious. Is that what you mean, Doctor?"

"He's only twelve years old, Golm. I meant he is becoming more aggressive, more difficult to control. He has developed a pronounced hostility toward me recently. His mother has been like a daughter to me, and he's almost like a son, but now he's deeply jealous of my relationship with his mother. I'm most concerned about his future, but I'm even more concerned about Sophia's emotional health."

"I can understand your concern, sir, and I'll be very careful in my conversation with Dr. Kara-Kash this evening. May I ask you one question?"

"Certainly."

"Dr. Morgan, at Hanover, mentioned a feud that developed in the press between old Dr. Stelgis Kara-Kash and an anthropologist named Brodermen. Can you tell me anything about this man?"

His expression changed suddenly, color drained from his face and I could see him tense. He took a deep, controlled breath, sipped his wine, then smiled, but I knew he was masking his real feelings. "What bearing could that old matter have on the present situation? Brodermen was a nothing, but he cost that great man the one thing he'd worked for all his life."

"I understand that, sir. Could you tell me if Brodermen's first name was Alfred?"

His face blanched, and his fingers tightened about the

stem of his glass until he gained control of himself and put it down on the bar. "What difference does his first name make?"

"I found three newspaper clippings in Stelgis' suitcase this morning, carefully hidden in the lining. One mentioned an unusual dinner given by the Adventurer's Club, at which frozen mastodon steak was served. It said that this had been provided by a member named Alfred Brodermen who was attached to the American Embassy in Moscow. I wondered if this could be the same man who had once been at the University of Pennsylvania."

"I don't remember offhand Brodermen's first name, but it couldn't have been the same man. What are you searching for, Golm?"

"Stelgis has expressed some rather bizarre ideas, as you know. On the basis of certain facts, I believe he has—"

"I really must leave now, Golm, but take seriously what I have told you. I want you to withdraw from this case as soon as possible. I insist upon it. Thank you for the drink."

"Don't you want to know what was in the other clippings?"

"Later, perhaps. I must run now." He slipped off the stool and started to leave, but stopped when I spoke.

"One more thing, sir. Dr. Karsloff said that you keep in touch with old Dr. Snyder, who used to be chief of Obs-Gyn. Do you know his address in Englewood?"

"No, I do not. I believe he lives in Florida now."

As he almost ran out of the restaurant, I felt certain that he had lied to me. I looked at my drink, untouched since Semminetti's arrival, and asked the bartender for fresh ice.

As I sipped the martini, I felt confused and uncertain. Dr. Semminetti was peculiar, but he was also an experienced psychiatrist, respected by his colleagues. I knew that he was deeply involved with Sophia Kara-Kash and her son and he might be correct in his conclusions about their problems. Who was I, a second-year resident, to question his judgment? But why had he departed so abruptly, and why hadn't he asked about the other clippings? Equally confusing, why had he bristled at the mention of Alfred Brodermen and my question about Dr. Snyder?

I glanced at my watch. It was still five minutes of seven. I went to the men's room. The public phone was on the wall, and there were several phone books on a shelf underneath. I turned on the light, found the Bergen County directory, opened it to the "S's" and went down the column until I came to "Snyder." There were several listed, but only a few for Englewood, and none with the usual "M.D." following the name.

My name was being called when I returned to the bar.

Chapter Eight

She was waiting at the entrance to the main dining room,
facing away from me as I approached. She was wearing a
beautifully tailored linen suit, the jacket of which enhanced her square shoulders and narrow waist. The fra-
grance of a subtle perfume rose from her hair as I stopped
behind her. The top of her head was even with my shoulder.

"Good evening, Dr. Kara-Kash."

She turned quickly, startled by my voice. "I—I'm sorry
I'm late, Doctor, I had trouble finding a taxi."

"No problem at all. I've only been here a few minutes."

I nodded at the headwaiter and he came with menus
to lead us to a table in the corner. I held her chair as she
sat down, then took the one to her right.

"You like a cocktail, sir?"

"Yes, please. What will you have, Dr. Kara-Kash?"

"Could I have a dry martini?" she asked.

"Make it two, waiter. On the rocks, please."

She seemed more interested in the menu than in me.
She seemed frightened.

"I was wondering where you would leave Stelgis this
evening. I could have come to your apartment."

"He has a friend in our building. They're watching

television. Would you please order for me, Dr. Golm? I'm not very hungry."

"How about some winter melon soup? Their pepper steak and steamed fish with ginger and scallions are very good. Perhaps we can share the dishes?"

"That will be fine. Stelgis always orders for us."

"He's a remarkable child, Dr. Kara-Kash. You must be very proud of him."

The waiter came with our drinks, relieving her of the necessity of replying. I picked up my drink, looked directly at her until she met my eyes, then lifted my glass. She picked up her drink, hesitated, then lifted it slightly. Her hand was trembling. I gave the hovering waiter our order. When he was gone, I raised my glass again, smiled and said, like an ass, "To your good health, Dr. Kara-Kash, and to Stelgis, may the programing be good this evening."

She sipped her drink, took a substantial swallow, then another. I finished my drink in a few gulps. "Finish it," I said, "and let's have another." I knew that she was grateful for my suggestion. She appeared very ill at ease and I knew that I shouldn't rush her.

She looked up at me, smiling for the first time after she had finished her second martini. The color had come up in her cheeks and her nervousness seemed to have abated. She continued to smile, then averted her eyes.

"I hope you've had a nice visit with Stelgis. He was so eager to see you."

"Yes," she said, hesitated, searched for the right words, then added, "we've discussed his problems at camp. I—I hope there will be no trouble about—"

"It's all been resolved up there, Doctor. The court order was only a formality and there will be no record made of it. We—the institute is part of the state's mental health system. The matter is now completely in our hands. You shouldn't be too concerned about this little episode. What are your plans? When will you be returning to Paris?"

"I've been excused from my commitment there. I—we plan to spend the rest of the summer here. I'm not due back at the university until September."

"Oh, that's good," I said. "I can continue my friendship with Stelgis. I've become very fond of him."

"I'm glad," she said, sincerely. "He adores you and your Korean friend. He doesn't usually respond well to strangers."

"Did he tell you about my friend's speech problem?"

A genuine smile came to her lips, the first natural one since her arrival. "Yes, he told me about the prosthesis you're planning. He wants to help you. It was an ingenious idea, Dr. Golm. I suspect it will work."

"It was Stelgis's idea," I said. "He's a remarkable child, with almost unlimited potential. Are there any questions you'd like to ask me about him?"

She sipped at her drink. I wondered if I dared order a third, but decided against it. The second seemed just right. She was beginning to relax.

"Dr. Karsloff telephoned me this afternoon, saying that you had some recommendations to make. What do you suggest, Doctor?"

"What do *you* feel would be best for him right now?" I asked.

"I think he feels most secure with me."

"My experience is limited, of course, but I've found that parents are not always the best judges of what may be best for their children. I believe that Stelgis may be at a critical stage in his emotional development—he needs perhaps to be more on his own—under proper supervision, of course."

"What would you suggest specifically, Doctor?"

"I think, and Dr. Karsloff agrees, that he could benefit from a good boarding school, where he could live with boys his own age."

"He's never been away from me. I—I know from personal experience just how traumatic it is to be separated from one's parent at an age when—"

"I don't believe he should be presented with such a challenge abruptly. He should be prepared for it, made to look forward to it as something he wants to do."

"How?"

"I'd like to help, Dr. Kara-Kash. I think that he trusts me. If you plan to spend the summer in New York, I'd like to spend time with him, perhaps on a weekly basis.

It shouldn't appear to be a doctor-patient relationship, but just as friends. I know that Dr. Karsloff would make time available to me. Perhaps we could do some fishing, go to a ball game, I could expose him to experiences he's missed. We might rent a car and visit some of the good schools. You could be part of it."

"You're very kind, Dr. Golm. I'd like to think about what you've said. We've not been apart since—"

"Do you like Chicago?"

"Not really. I've always looked on the medical center here as home."

"Do you have tenure at Chicago?"

"Yes, but that isn't important. I—" She stopped talking as the waiter brought our soup. When he was gone, she said, "I've thought of coming back. That's why I've kept the apartment."

"Why don't you? I'm sure Dr. Karsloff could be helpful. And Dr. Semminetti."

The suggestion of a frown came to her face. She started to speak, then stopped.

"Could it be that Dr. Semminetti might be one of Stelgis's problems? He—I got the impression that Stelgis may be somewhat hostile."

"I was not thinking entirely of Stelgis's welfare."

I kept my eyes on my soup, trying not to show undue interest in what she was trying to say. She tasted the soup, then began to eat it, using it, I thought, as a diversion. We remained silent until the waiter served our main course, dividing the two dishes on each of our plates.

"It's delicious," she said. "Tell me a bit about yourself, Dr. Golm. Stelgis was fascinated by some of the things you told him about your childhood in Indiana."

I knew that that she was using me and my past to direct me away from her problems, but she was sincerely interested when I told her about the year I'd spent working as a copywriter in an ad agency when I'd thought of becoming a writer. I told her about my father and grandfather, the roles they had played in our town, about my mother and her greenhouse, about my rebellion and reluctance to follow Father into medicine.

"Do you like psychiatry, now that you're well into it?"

"Yes, very much. I guess I'm more interested in what

happened to people's minds than their bodies. I'd have made a lousy family doctor."

"I doubt that. Their patients have emotional problems, too. Didn't I read that six out of ten patients who go to them have symptoms for which no organic explanation can be found?"

"That's true, but my grandfather's and father's acts would have been hard to follow. Grandfather was educated and trained in Germany, and came to Indiana when he was a young man. My father really wanted to become a surgeon, but I've always suspected he lacked the courage. He became a good general physician, and he's had a happy life. Most of us, I'm coming to believe, can adjust to whatever course our lives take. I hope so. I'm thinking of giving my next two years of training to child psychiatry. There are so few child psychiatrists, and the need is so great. I've even toyed with the idea of returning to Indiana and affiliating with one of the new mental health complexes. There's one just getting under way in Bordentown, where I grew up. It will serve a five-county area."

She was watching my face closely as I talked. I hadn't meant to reveal so much about myself, and I felt self-conscious, suddenly at a loss for words.

"I'm so glad I came this evening," she said. "I almost didn't, after—I find it so difficult to meet strangers. You're so easy to talk to."

"Dr. Semminetti may not be one of my great admirers," I said, sure that she'd hesitated, about to tell me something important. "Dr. Semminetti is so fond of both you and Stelgis—he feels responsible for your welfare."

"Yes, I know. He was all I had to turn to when Father died. I owe so much to him. Father and I were very close. My mother was ill much of the time when I was a young child."

"He was a very great man. It was so unfortunate that you lost him when you were so young. How old were you?"

"Seventeen. I had an aunt, a teacher, who came to live with me. She died when I was twenty. Then there was only Uncle Ted—but I'm talking too much about my problems. I want to think about what you've said about Stelgis. I really don't care for dessert, and I must get back to Stelgis."

I had wanted to ask if Stelgis had told her about his experience in the Bronx last evening, but knew that this was not the time to introduce complicating problems in a relationship that had developed far better than I had hoped.

We walked outside and waited until a cab appeared. I waved and he pulled to the curb, stopping in front of us. She turned to me. Tears were brimming in her eyes. I offered my hand as she thanked me. She took it. When I pressed it ever so slightly, she pulled it away quickly, turning to enter the taxi. The door slammed and I was suddenly alone, still feeling the warmth of her hand. I felt confused, more alone than before. Poor wounded, frightened Sophia, so beautiful, so much in need of love and understanding—crippled by two old men and a child she loved but could not understand.

I waited for the light, then crossed over the subway entrance, stepping around a hallucinating old wino who sat with his paper bag on the first step.

It was after nine when I got back to the tower. Jimmy was still at the desk, filling in for Yong Ha. He handed me two telephone slips. I took them and went up to my apartment without looking at them until I'd hung my clothes in the closet. One was from Margaret Bochmeir, the other from Lieutenant MacMann, of the New York Police Department. Each asked that I call when I got in.

I called Margaret first at Hadley Hall. My feelings toward her, for some reason I could not explain, had changed. I felt only a sense of shame for the cheap, shabby thing I'd done. When she answered, sleep in her voice, I said, "Hi, sorry I wasn't in when you called. And I'm sorry about last night."

"That's all right, Gus. I'm still half awake. What a day. Two hypermanics came in late and were they ever wild."

"What's on your mind?"

"We talked about going to Lincoln Center tomorrow night—Makarova's *Giselle*. Would you mind very much if we didn't go?"

"Not a bit. I'm on receiving tomorrow and may have to be on stand-by call in the evening."

"How's your patient?"

"With his mother, thank goodness. I'm really sorry I was rude last night."

"Gus, I've been thinking about us."

"What are you trying to say?"

"Maybe things have become too intense. Maybe we should just cool it for a while and think about things. What do you think?"

"Perhaps you're right."

"We'd love to have you come to dinner on Friday, though. We're inviting several people."

"I'll make it if I can."

"Good night, Gus."

"Good night."

I thought for some time after putting down the phone. Had she seen through the shabby thing Charley and I had tried to pull, or was she simply giving me an easy way out after sensing my feelings? In either event, I felt depressed.

I dialed the number Lieutenant MacMann had left.

"MacMann speaking."

"This is Dr. Golm at the medical center. You asked me to call."

"Oh, yes, Doctor. Thanks for getting back. I'm off duty now, at home, but could I stop by in the morning for a few minutes?"

"Yes, of course. Could you tell me what about?"

"It's nothing that can't wait until morning."

I explained that I'd be working the receiving floor at the institute after eight and told him how to get there.

I turned on the tube, switching from channel to channel, bored by its dreary offerings, feeling restless and depressed. I finally went into the bedroom. A full moon was shining through the east window. A cool easterly breeze was blowing in off Long Island Sound.

I set my alarm and crawled in between the sheets and waited for sleep.

Chapter Nine

I woke as usual before my alarm went off on Wednesday morning, wondering why I oversleep only when I do not set it. I started to make coffee, then decided to go to the institute's dining room for breakfast. I showered, shaved and began to dress, still feeling depressed, thinking of my upcoming interview with Lieutenant Mac-Mann. His purpose in coming to me would only mean that he had new information on the Peroni boy's death and that such information was related to Steglis. If the boy had to be subjected to police interrogation, it would probably adversely affect my relationship with him. Even more important, it would be equally traumatic for his mother. Still thinking of the new problems that might arise, I donned my whites and walked down to the institute shortly after seven.

As I came off the line with my tray and started for an empty table at the back of the room, I noticed Dr. Karsloff sitting alone at a table near the window. When he beckoned with his head for me to join him, I changed course and went to sit down across from him, sure that he had come here specifically to talk with me. He had only coffee and a half-eaten doughnut in front of him, looking at my loaded tray with something close to disgust in his eyes.

"My God, Golm, do you eat that much at every meal?"

"Breakfast, yes. We often miss lunch on receiving."

"And you never seem to gain a pound. I starve myself and fight the scale every week. I was hoping to catch you this morning."

"I had a very good talk with Dr. Kara-Kash. She—"

"I don't give a damn about that now, Golm! Why don't you learn to shut up and listen? No wonder Falstein wants to turn you over to someone else."

"I'm sorry, sir."

He sipped his coffee, thought for a moment, then said, "Your present appointment here is up on the fifteenth. Have you given any serious thoughts to your future?"

"Yes, sir. I'd like to qualify in child psychiatry, or at least get some experience in that area. I've appreciated very much my training here in general psychiatry."

"What do you really want to do when you go out on your own? Falstein says he's never been able to find out, except that you seem to want to return to Indiana. He finds that hard to understand. So do I."

I felt twinges of anger beginning to stir in me again.

"Most New Yorkers still believe the world ends at Hoboken," I said. "People have problems in Indiana, too. I've been thinking about that map in the dean's office— with all the pins showing where alumni located. Almost eighty per cent are practicing in a few big eastern cities or California. They see maybe three hundred patients a year, get seventy-five to a hundred dollars for their fifty-minute hour, play a lot of golf and get referrals from G.P.'s who are glad to get rid of their frightened executives and unfulfilled housewives. I don't want any of that."

"Well, well, it's not quite that bleak. I never dreamed you ever looked at that map. What the hell *do* you want?"

"I've thought about affiliating with one of the new federally sponsored community mental health centers. In fact, there's one being built in my hometown that will serve a five-county area."

"What got you to thinking in that direction?"

"That's where psychiatric skills are needed most. Have you really read that report by the President's Committee for Mental Health?"

"For Chrissake, Golm, I helped write it! Go on, tell me more."

"I believe psychiatry has earned the shabby reputation it has in general medicine and surgery. Most doctors look on us about the same way they look on chiropractors. They all need our help, but either won't ask for it or are afraid to. I think our greatest challenge lies in public and professional education. Mental illness is our biggest health problem. The new centers are intended to educate and train teachers, policemen, judges, clergymen, even physicians and nurses, to help them recognize early symptoms and get patients prompt treatment."

"That's very interesting, Golm," he said, reaching over to pick two of the three strips of crisp bacon from my plate. He continued to smile as he nibbled at them. "What would you say if I told you that our appointment policies at the institute were changed during my tenure as director to appoint twenty per cent of our applicants from the hinterlands? That's how you got your appointment, if you want to know."

"It's a good policy, but I notice most of your residents by the final year forget where they came from and head for the easy money. Half of the staffs in our state hospitals are made up of foreign doctors or old G.P.'s on political appointments, most of them without any psychiatric training at all. One of these days we're going to get a national health program and they'll start telling us what and where we can practice. Maybe it's time."

"My God, Golm, you're beginning to sound like an evangelical preacher at a camp meeting. What's changed your thinking so suddenly?"

"It hasn't been sudden. I keep thinking of my old man, the way he's spent his life. He sees thirty or forty patients a day, makes hospital rounds, serves on the school board and hasn't had a vacation as long as I can remember."

"All right, I have a proposition to make. At the end of your two-year residency, you are presumably qualified to practice general psychiatry and eventually to apply for board certification. We can offer you a fellowship in child psychiatry for another two years, upon your agreement to give at least five years to community health in a non-urban area. There is federal and other grant money available to pay you substantially more than you now get as a resident. Well, Golm?"

"Sounds great, sir. I'd appreciate the opportunity."

"All right, your appointment is only a formality. You can start the middle of this month. Falstein and I have worked out a program for you. He thinks you'll be up to it."

"I—I don't know what to say. I thought Dr. Falstein disliked me, I thought he felt I had wasted his time."

"He does, for Chrissake, Golm! But he's a good psychiatrist and teacher, he recognizes your potential and can sublimate personal feelings. Not a bad model for you to follow."

"What is the program, sir?"

"Well, we just happen to have a few new chores that need to be done and no one on the attending staff available to do them. Those bastards in Albany and at the National Institute for Mental Health have been after us to set up a consulting service for general physicians throughout the state. Falstein said you once had ambitions to become a writer. Most of us live by jargon, using a language that even we can't understand at times. I've read some of your papers. You write passably well. We now have in our computer the names and addresses of every family doctor, internist and surgeon now practicing in New York. We want you to give your mornings to preparing a monthly newsletter that will be mailed to them regularly. One section will be devoted to questions submitted by readers. You'll provide the answers. I want—"

"But sir, do you think I'm qualified to—"

"Of course you're not, but you can find the right answers. You'll have our staff to consult. The newsletter will also keep readers informed of our new research and new treatment modalities, with occasional case histories of patients with problems most likely to be first seen by a general physician. You should be able to handle this mornings. You can give your afternoons to the children's outpatient service and our inpatient adolescent ward. We'll expect you to give your evenings to community education. We're always getting requests for speakers to address local groups on mental health—churches, synagogues, P.T.A. meetings. You would also act as a consultant on call to the three schools in our immediate vicinity. You'll submit to me a written monthly report of your activities and—"

"But, sir—it seems too much for a single person. I'll be—"

"Yes, you will. I'm glad you've helped us resolve a problem that has worried us. It's agreed then?"

"Dr. Karsloff, I appreciate your confidence in me, but I'll have to have some help—"

"What makes you think I have confidence in you, Golm? I think, by God, you'll probably make a mess of it, but I don't have anyone else to do it. If you get too overloaded, I may be able to get some volunteer help from our house staff. Okay?"

"I'll do my best."

"Good. I have to go to another damned meeting now. Oh, yes—I'm taking you off receiving. Would you like the next ten days as vacation time? No need to answer that. Don't go away, though. I called Sophia last night. She has some important decisions to make. Help her all you can."

I sat there too stunned to move. I finished my coffee and went down to the duty roster. My name had been replaced on receiving by one of the revolving interns from the hospital's medical service. Of one thing I was certain: on receiving he would certainly learn how to do the neurological examination. Feeling as free as a bird, I went to the receiving center to see if Lieutenant MacMann had arrived. He was waiting for me in the visitor's room, talking with our security officer, who nodded toward me as I entered.

"I'm MacMann, Dr. Golm," he said, coming toward me with his hand outstretched. "I'll only take a minute of your time. Can we talk here?"

"Sure. Visitors won't be coming in for another hour or so. What's on your mind?"

I nodded to the security guard and he left the room, closing the door behind him.

"You've undoubtedly read the papers and heard news reports on the Peroni boy's murder on Monday evening."

"Yes I have," I said, offering nothing more.

Lieutenant MacMann was in his middle thirties. He had curious, intelligent eyes that seemed to be judging me as he continued to smile.

"It's always nice getting an opportunity to revisit the medical center," he said. "I and all of my sisters were born here, and I owe my life to Children's Hospital. Had meningitis when I was seven. They gave me that new vaccine that was developed here—"

"Bacitracin?" I asked.

"Something like that." He pointed to a strip of scar tissue on his cheek. "That was treated in your old emergency room."

"Knife or something else?"

"A little present from a Saturday-night special, when I was on patrol duty in Washington Heights. They wanted me to come back and see a plastic surgeon, but I never seemed able to find time. Know old Dr. Phillip Snyder who used to be here? He delivered all of us. We still get a birthday card from him every year. I guess not many care that much about their patients anymore."

"Some of them still do," I said. "Dr. Snyder retired as chief of service some time ago."

"Yes, I know. Lives with his daughter's family over in Englewood. Had his card last week. I was a Fourth of July baby. But I'm wasting your time. What I came about is just routine. I have the Peroni case. I drove up to Hanover yesterday. The Peroni kid had been in camp there, but was sent home the Saturday before he was killed. I had a talk with the director, and learned he'd had some trouble with another boy. I stopped at the state hospital to talk to the superintendent. He said this boy—name of Kara-Kash—was a—well, a disturbed kid. Said you'd come up there to get him and bring him back to New York."

"Yes, that's true. He's with his mother at present."

He waited for me to elaborate, but I remained silent.

"I learned that this boy had made some threats against the Peroni kid—and well, we have to follow every lead. What I want to know, doctor, is this—do you know if this Kara-Kash kid could have been in the upper Bronx around eight to nine o'clock Monday evening?"

I suddenly remembered one of the important things

I'd learned from the time I had spent in emergency rooms as an intern and resident: You never deliberately withhold information from the police when questioned about a potential court case, but you never volunteer information, unless to confirm what the interrogator already knows.

"Do you suspect the Kara-Kash boy was in that area?"

"Well, we actually know he was there. We hauled some street kids in for questioning, maybe scared them a little. We took a very expensive watch from one of them and a jacket that the camp director identified as belonging to the Kara-Kash boy."

"All right, Lieutenant, I'll tell you what I know, but I'm quite certain that this boy had nothing whatever to do with the killing."

"Thank you, Doc. I don't believe he did either, but I have to get all the information I can."

I gave him a complete accounting of my experience with Stelgis, from the time I'd picked him up at Hanover until I'd delivered him to his mother. I then explained that his mother was also close to being emotionally disturbed and that I hoped he could spare her and her son a public police investigation, which would be picked up by the media.

He looked at me, holding my eyes, as he said, "I appreciate your concern, Doc, but this is murder. You'd never believe how many parents refuse to admit that their kids are dangerous hoodlums. I've got to talk to them. I've already had a talk with Dr. Semminetti."

"How did you come to question him?"

"The director said he had visited the boy at camp several times, that he was an old and close friend of his family. He wanted to protect them, just as you do, but he was cooperative when I insisted."

"In what way?"

"Well, he said this boy has had the run of the Museum of Natural History during his vacations. The murder weapon—that dart and blowgun—came from the museum. He also said that this kid and the Peroni boy had fought and threats were made. What would you suggest I do, if you were in my place?"

"You have to get all the evidence you can, of course,"

I said, "but didn't you say you didn't believe the boy had killed Peroni?"

"Yes, I did, and I still don't."

"Why do you say that?"

"There's more to this case than just another street gang killing. That's a really tough neighborhood and any of those kids are capable of killing, but they were up on White Plains Road at the time of Peroni's death, and had come in a group down to Gun Hill when they saw the Kara-Kash boy and rolled him. In my work, you get to know these kids, and you can tell when they're lying. I'm going from here to talk again with the Peroni boy's family. I have a search warrant, if they refuse to let me go through his personal belongings."

"When do you plan to talk to the Kara-Kash boy and his mother?"

"As soon as I can. I was hoping you'd help me."

"In what way?"

"Perhaps by telling me where I can find them."

"But they have an apartment in Dr. Semminetti's building—"

"Yes, I know, but they took off last night, in a cab—with their suitcases. Can you tell me where they might have gone?"

"No, I honestly can't, but I'll do all I can to help locate them. The mother, as I told you, is very emotional, and panics easily. I'll find her and convince her that she should co-operate with you. I beg you not to release the information you have to the press. It will only complicate things more."

"That's what Dr. Semminetti said. He's promised to co-operate in every way possible. Seemed like a nice man, and he was as concerned about the mother as you are." He removed his card from his pocket, wrote two numbers on the back and handed it to me. "You can reach me at one of these numbers around the clock. Let me know at once when you locate them."

"I'll do that, Lieutenant, and thank you for being so honest with me."

I watched him leave, feeling increasingly anxious as I went up to the ninth floor to Dr. Semminetti's office.

"Is he in?" I asked his secretary.

"Oh, no, Dr. Golm," she said. "He left for Chicago this morning, real early."

I went back to the elevator and up to the top floor. Miss Thomas looked up at me in surprise as I entered the waiting room. "He's not back from his meeting, Dr. Golm. He's tied up most of the morning, and—"

"I'll wait," I said.

He came in shortly after ten, accompanied by two attendings. "I can't see you now, Golm."

"I only need a minute or two."

"Go on in, gentlemen," he said, "I'll join you later. . . . Well, Golm, I hope you don't make a habit of this."

I walked out into the hallway. He followed me, his attitude changing when I told him of my meeting with Lieutenant MacMann and of Dr. Kara-Kash's disappearance with her son. "I'm certain they've returned to Chicago, sir," I said.

"Why do you assume that?"

"Dr. Semminetti left for Chicago early this morning. He—I'm certain he's not the best person to convince her she should return with the boy at once."

"My God, Golm, he's practically raised her—the only person who's ever been close to her."

"She's developed a deep antagonism to him; I know that from last night. You asked me to stick around on my vacation, but I'd like very much to visit my father and mother, to tell them about my new appointment. I could fly to Chicago first and try to talk to Dr. Kara-Kash, then rent a car for the trip home. She really must return to New York with the boy. The lieutenant doesn't believe Stelgis killed the Peroni kid, but he knows for sure that he was in the vicinity—"

"I think you're shooting from the hip, Golm. Semminetti apparently knows the score, and he'll convince her that she should return. In the meantime, I have a suggestion to make."

"Yes, sir."

"About your newsletter. The institute of the hospital of the University of Pennsylvania received a grant last year similar to ours. They've had their newsletter out for several months. A Dr. Felix Pollatan is editing it. I want you to go down and talk to him. You can put a voucher in for your expences. I'd take the train; it's quicker and less expensive. If Semminetti doesn't convince Sophia that she should return, maybe you can go out and talk to her."

"But, sir, I thought I'd—"

"Dr. Pollatan is expecting you at ten tomorrow morning. I talked to him this morning. Don't keep him waiting."

"Yes, sir."

I went down to the street, heading for my apartment. I stopped at the corner, remembering something, then cut over to the medical school, going to its alumni office in the basement.

Mrs. Vos was most helpful. Yes, Dr. Phillip Snyder was an alumnus of the medical school. Yes, she had his address in Englewood and his telephone number. She checked her index file and gave me the information.

I walked back to the tower and went up to my apartment to change from my whites to slacks and a sports shirt, intending to go to the library and look through medical newsletters on file there, but it was a beautiful day, just warm enough to make indoors seem oppressive. Although I'd been handed my first vacation in two years, I felt certain that since I'd been asked to stick around, Dr. Karsloff probably already had plans, and had made certain I'd be available.

On impulse, I went to my phone and dialed the number Mrs. Vos had given me for Dr. Snyder. There were several rings and I was ready to hang up when he answered, in a petulent, sleepy voice. I felt certain he had been napping.

"Dr. Snyder speaking," he said. "My daughter is not here, my grandson, my grandaughter, the maid and my son-in-law are out. Now stop bothering me."

"This is Dr. Golm, at the medical center, sir."

"Who did you say?" he asked.

"Dr. Golm. I'm at the Psychiatric Institute."

"Well now, that's different. Sorry if I was rude. This damned phone's been ringing every ten minutes. What's on your mind, Doctor? I didn't think anybody from over there knew I was alive these days."

"Oh, but they do. I've heard a lot of nice things about you, Doctor. We have a very unusual case here at the institute; I believe you delivered him. Dr. Karsloff told me that you might be willing to talk to me about him."

"Well now, how is Leon?"

"He's fine, still fighting Albany. I was wondering if you could spare a few minutes."

"My boy, I have most of each day to spare these last five years. I'll be glad to see you—any time."

"How about this afternoon, sir? I could come at your convenience. Perhaps you could even have lunch with me."

"That's damned nice of you, Doctor. I'd love to get out of this place for lunch. Come on over."

He gave me his address, told me the bus number to take from the bridge station, and said he had a car, but I would have to drive it to the restaurant. I wrote the number down, then looked at the clock. It was almost ten.

As I put the phone down, I noticed an envelope lying on my desk. Written in Yong Ha's hand was a note, in proper English: "I couldn't find anything by Dr. Brodermen but two or three recent publications by Dr. Sophia Kara-Kash. I'll find them in the journals, if you want me to."

I removed the sheet of paper from the envelope and found three listings from the Indexus Medicus. One was in the Winter issue of the *Illinois State Medical Journal: Blood Factors Differentiated in Schizophrenic Patients*.

I wrote: "Thanks, Yong, if you have time, would you get the paper I've underlined. Xerox a copy from the journal. No rush. See you this evening."

Chapter Ten

I caught a number twelve bus and rode it on its circuitous route through Englewood Cliffs, Leonia and the edge of Tenafly, finally arriving in downtown Englewood. I caught a local taxi and gave the driver Dr. Snyder's address.

We turned into a tree-lined street with beautiful land-scaped homes on either side, that ended in a cul-de-sac and turnaround circle. Dr. Snyder was in the center house on the circle. I paid the cabbie and walked toward the front door. There was a glassed-in sun porch on the right. Its door opened and Dr. Snyder motioned me to come around on the connecting flagstone walk.

"Come on in, Doctor. I'll be ready in a few minutes."

He looked exactly like Colonel Sanders, a portly, neat old man with snow-white hair that was matched with a white mustache and goatee. "You don't have to say it, Doctor. Even my grandchildren and their friends call me the chicken colonel. Sit down and make yourself comfortable. God, I'm glad you called. I was just finishing my most important work these days." He nodded toward four file-card boxes on a table by the window. "I delivered more than three thousand babies during my career and I remember every damned one of them, but sometimes I forget where they keep the damned bathrooms around here. My old vessels are becoming sclerosed with each passing day."

I glanced at a stack of engraved cards lying on the table beside the boxes.

He noticed, appearing a little embarrassed, but said, "I send every damned one of them a birthday card. I always put a note on them. I don't know why I keep sending them. There used to be a reason. I sent a little begging appeal every Christmas for gifts to my research fund, and it brought in as much as twenty-five thousand dollars some years. Got five thousand every year from one of the Rockefellers. Now I do it, I guess, just to prove to somebody that I'm still alive."

"It's a wonderful thing to do, sir. My dad does the same thing. He and my grandfather delivered half the babies in our county, back in Indiana."

"And many of them in their parents' own bed, I'll bet, at least in the old days. Probably had a lower infection rate than their hospitals have now."

"That's right. They used to place them on old newspapers instead of clean sheets."

"And for a damned good reason! That printer's ink had an effective bactericidal action. Too many lazy doctors depending on antibiotics too long—the bugs become immune before new ones can be discovered."

Still mumbling, he went into the house and returned a few minutes later, wearing a natty red sports jacket, holding a set of keys and the signal box for the electric garage doors. He handed the keys to me and I followed him around the front of the house to the four-car garage. There was a beautiful old Cadillac, brightly polished, as immaculate as the day it had come off the line (about 1950).

"I think we might go up to Louie's Restaurant on Nine W. It's on the corner at Palisades Avenue. Good German food. Does that interest you?"

"You can bet it does. I hope they have sauerbraten and red cabbage."

"It's a specialty of the house."

The old man continued to talk as we drove up the long hill toward the restaurant, asking questions about my work at the institute, my father and grandfather, old friends in the various departments of the medical center, and I realized that he was starved for companionship.

We parked behind the restaurant, which was only a block from the river and the Palisades, going into it up a back stairway. The headwaiter recognized him and became solicitous, taking us to a booth in an alcove.

"Well, Doctor," the old man said, "tell me about this patient that's giving you so many problems." He watched my face, waiting, and I knew he was eager to become involved in medicine again.

"Do you remember old Dr. Kara-Kash?" I asked.

"Stelgis? Who could forget him? Absolutely insane, but probably the only genius I've ever known."

"My patient is his grandson."

The merest suggestion of a frown touched his face. He sipped his drink, then said, "Must be grown up by now. No, he was the last one I delivered, back in the late sixties, a week before I retired. She had a difficult time, poor thing. He weighed almost nine pounds, far too large for her size, but she didn't come to me until the sixth month. I really exploded at that arrogant little poop Semminetti, who was responsible for her. I remember the child developed severe dermatitis, and had a hard time adjusting to his formula. I wanted to turn her over to a pediatrician, but she insisted that I continue to see her. What was her name?"

"Sophia."

"Oh, yes. She wasn't married, refused to—" He paused to sip his drink again, and I suspected he'd lost his chain of thought, but it wasn't forgetfulness: he was suddenly remembering professional ethics.

"She had a bad episode a year or so before this child was born. I never got all of the details, except what that fool Semminetti told me, but he . . . I've made it a practice during my career to not talk about my patients. I have a feeling you didn't come to see me without good reasons. Tell me what you're up against. I'll help you if I can."

He listened attentively as I told him in detail.

"My goodness," he said. "Have you reached any conclusions about this child's bizarre claims?"

"Yes, sir, I have. I believe, based on the various bits of information I gave you—the news clippings, his statements under Pentothal, Dr. Semminetti's interest in his anthropometric measurements, his mother's and Dr. Semminetti's evasions about who his father might have been —well, I believe he thinks his mother somehow obtained viable sperm from an Ice Age man, was artificially impregnated and delivered him."

"It's absolutely fantastic," the old man said. "I haven't thought about it in years, but it's beginning to make sense to me now."

He looked away from me, avoiding my eyes for some time, then sipped at his drink. "It couldn't happen, dammit! I headed the Institute for the Study of Human Reproduction for the last ten years that I was chief of the Obs-Gyn Service and I know damn well that it couldn't." I waited, not daring to intrude on his thoughts. "Yes, a lot of it is beginning to make sense—why she never sought prenatal care until the sixth month. Why she refused to discuss her baby's father. Goddamn that old man! I must have your word, Doctor, on your honor, that you'll never discuss with another person what I'm about to tell you—not Leon Karsloff, Semminetti, the boy's mother or the boy."

"You have my word, sir. My interest is only in helping the child and his mother."

"I believe you, son. God, it comes back now like it happened yesterday. I can still see the wild look on his face."

"Old Dr. Kara-Kash's face, sir?"

"Yes. He came to one of my young residents at the institute with a specimen of frozen human sperm—conned the youngster into running a test on it to see that it was viable. It was damned viable. Inadvertently, he let slip to my resident that this was probably the most important sperm sample on earth. We had another madman in research at our institute at the time, and this man, unbeknownst to me or any of my attending staff, was actually hiring women for experimentation—poor, ignorant black women. He was a physiologist, not an M.D., but was working nights in a laboratory here in Jersey. He managed somehow to impregnate one woman—but she almost died from infection of her tubes. She had been a charity patient at our outpatient clinic and talked. We ran this man out of medicine, and would have prosecuted him had we dared, but we'd have been forced to admit that he was on our staff, making us equally liable. We saved the woman, covered it up, but—"

"But what, sir?" I asked when he seemed to be losing his thread of thought.

"When I had him in for the showdown, he told me that Kara-Kash was as guilty as he was—that he was about to do something even worse. It wasn't easy, let me tell you, but I got it out of Kara-Kash. He had placed an ad in the help-wanted columns of a large black newspaper, seeking a healthy, mature woman to bear a child, offering ten thousand dollars. I was able to kill the ad the morning it was to appear. The man was absolutely astounded when I explained that he could be prosecuted for human experimentation, lose his appointment at the medical center, negate all the brilliant work he had done."

"I presume he was going to impregnate the woman with the frozen sperm."

"That's it exactly."

"Do you know what became of the sperm?"

"He told me that he had destroyed it. I assumed that he had."

"You didn't learn where he'd obtained it."

"No. Actually, I didn't want to know. We had just been successful in developing new fertility drugs, which today, unfortunately, are producing multiple births. The reputation not only of the institute was always at stake, but also the university's and the National Institute's, which was giving us grant money."

"Dr. Morgan, clinical director up at Hanover State Hospital, worked in Dr. Kara-Kash's laboratory. He said the old man used to bring his daughter to work with him regularly. Do you think she would have been familiar with his plans?"

"I was afraid you'd ask that. Of course she knew. I suspect Semminetti might have known, too. He was always over there in those days. Can't stand the man."

"Do you think—I know this is a ridiculous question—but do you think the daughter might have impregnated herself with that sperm?"

"It's not a difficult procedure, as you know, Dr. Golm. She had premed and a year of medical school. She could have impregnated herself, or had someone do it for her. But it's just too fantastic to believe."

"Would Dr. Kara-Kash have kept records of the work he was doing in this area? I know she's kept all his papers in bound volumes."

"He never threw anything away. He was a sad, bitter old man after they passed him the second time for the Nobel. She was all he had—no wonder she was strange. Oh, my God—I forgot to call my daughter. They'll have every cop in Bergen County out looking for me."

"I can't tell you, sir, how much I appreciate your sharing this information with me. I'll make certain that it doesn't come back to embarrass you."

We went out to the car and I drove him home, stopping suddenly beside a taxi that was discharging a passenger at Palisades Avenue. I opened the window, asked if he would follow to pick me up. He would.

I parked the car back in his garage, refused his daughter's invitation to come in, said good-bye, thanked him for a wonderful afternoon, then went out to the waiting cab and asked him to take me all the way to the medical center.

I was still in something close to shock when I got out at the tower and went up to my apartment. It was one of the most fantastic afternoons I could remember. I had information that boggled even my mind, but it could explain, as nothing else could, the terrible tragedy that I'd sensed in Sophia Kara-Kash.

I'd nursed my beers carefully over the afternoon, so I mixed myself a very dry martini and sat down to try and sort out the thoughts that still clouded my mind. One thing was certain, though: Stelgis had very good reasons for believing himself to be the son of an Ice Age man.

I finished the drink, then decided to walk down to the staff room and see if anyone was there. As I was ready to leave, my telephone rang. It was Dr. Semminetti.

"Hello, Golm," he said. "Tried to get you earlier."

"I've been home only a short time."

"I came in from Chicago this afternoon. Did Lieutenant MacMann contact you?"

"Yes, I talked with him this morning. He knows that Stelgis was in the area when the Peroni boy was killed."

"I know. He just left. It looks very bad for the child. We can thank you for that. How in the world could you have let the boy out of your sight?"

"You know him far better than I do, Doctor. The doorman of your building told me he often got away from you, and his mother. I hope that Dr. Kara-Kash realizes that she must bring Stelgis back to New York."

"They are driving her car through and will be in late tomorrow. I hope, Golm, that you now know why I talked to you as I did last evening. Get yourself relieved of this case as soon as you can."

"Dr. Semminetti," I said, as he was about to hang up, "about old Dr. Snyder. He doesn't live in Florida, as you thought. He lives with his daughter's family over in Englewood."

"Why are you so interested in Dr. Snyder, Golm?"

"I thought I would have a talk with him."

"About what?"

I took a shot in the dark. "About his experiences with Dr. Kara-Kash. He delivered Stelgis, you know."

The connection was broken abruptly.

I sat for several minutes after putting down the phone, still trying to place all the facts that I had uncovered in order. Whatever young Stelgis might have learned about the circumstances of his birth, Dr. Semminetti also knew them. If Sophia Kara-Kash had gone through a breakdown after losing her father, she would probably have wanted more than anything else in the world to carry on his work. Her judgment could have been impaired—she was still very young and wouldn't have weighed risks to herself. Now she had to live with what she had done.

I suddenly remembered the card Lieutenant MacMann had given me, removed it from by billfold and decided to call him.

"This is Dr. Golm at the medical center," I said. "I've just learned that Dr. Kara-Kash will return with her son late tomorrow. They're driving back from Chicago."

"Yes, Dr. Golm, I learned that from Dr. Semminetti. There have been new developments in the Peroni case. For the time being, I will forgo interrogating the child and his mother. Dr. Semminetti confirmed what you said, that she's very close to being emotionally ill and—"

"I'm relieved to hear that, Lieutenant."

"We have some good leads, but—well it takes evidence to convict, even when you're sure of your killer."

"I'm curious, Lieutenant. You said you were pretty sure that the Kara-Kash boy wasn't responsible. I'll be seeing him when he returns. I was wondering if you still—"

"This if off the record, Dr. Golm, and I hope you won't repeat it, because it hasn't been released to the press. The cab driver who picked the boy up at your place and drove him to the Bronx has come forward with some information which pretty much exonerates him."

"Oh, thank God. And thank you for telling me."

"I knew how concerned you were. And thank you for calling me."

I walked down to the institute, feeling much relieved.

Chapter Eleven

I caught the eight o'clock train at Penn Station, but we lost thirty minutes in a tie-up outside of Newark, and it was ten-thirty when I reached the Thirtieth Street Station in Philadelphia, where I caught a taxi. Dr. Pollatan had been waiting for me, but he didn't seem upset.

"I assumed you would take the eight o'clock train," he said. "We've learned to accept delays since the federal government got into the act. Not like the old Pennsy."

He was an older man, probably in his sixties.

"I had a coronary two years ago, damned near died," he said, "then went for a by-pass last winter. Feel like a different man, but my doctor still wants me to take it easy. I could retire now, but there's a challenge in trying to educate doctors to the needs of mental patients. And what I suspect is even more important, to help them recognize and treat emotional problems that complicate the recovery of medical and surgical patients. Doctor, if you don't mind. I'll leave you here in my office with our back issues. The correspondence we've received is very interesting. It's all in that file cabinet."

After he had gone to his meeting, promising to come back and have lunch with me, I went through his back issues. He wrote in a stilted, verbose style, using all the clichés and jargon for which psychiatrists are noted. I thought of my father reading such material and knew that it would go into his wastebasket before he read more than a few lines. The type was too small, the layout was crowded and there were few photographs. He called his publication *The I.H.P. Report.* I knew that I could do better than that. Of one thing I was certain: the word "psychiatry" should not be mentioned. It should be something like *Emotional Problems in General Practice.*

Dr. Pollatan returned shortly before noon. "Where would you like to eat, Doctor? We have some fine restaurants. I've plenty of time."

"I've heard that Bookbinders has great seafood."

"Yes, we have two Bookbinders these days; I like the one in Center City best."

We took a cab to the restaurant. I complimented him on his newsletter, told him how much I appreciated his help and invited him to visit our institute.

"I don't write very well," he said, "and I'm still experimenting. I'll be glad to see your publication when it's available. Put me on your mailing list."

When we were seated in the rather old-fashioned restaurant, I took his home address, then said, as we waited for our fish, that he might help me with a problem that involved one of my patients.

"Back in the middle sixties, or thereabouts, there was a professor, or perhaps an instructor, in anthropology at your university. Name of Brodermen. His first name might be Alfred. How would I go about trying to contact him?"

"That's easy," he said. "Let me call a dean I know over there. I'll do it now. They're very slow in this restaurant, but it's worth waiting for."

He went to a public phone in the bar area, returning a short time later. "Yeah, he used to be here," he said, "but there's something funny about it. I got the impression that John didn't want to talk about it. I told him it involved a patient up in New York, and he loosened up a little. He'll see you if you want to go over there at two. I can drop you off on the way back, unless you want to talk to me more about your project."

"No, I got what I came for. You've been most helpful."

The fish *was* worth waiting for, and so was the baked Alaska. We left shortly before two and caught a cab outside; he dropped me off at the School of General Studies.

"John Sterling's office is just inside the front entrance, on the right," he said. "Nice to have met you, and I may take you up on that invitation to visit you."

Dean Sterling was also in his early sixties, a genial, outgoing man who was undoubtedly very good with students. "I understand you're interested in a former member of our faculty," he said, after I had introduced myself.

"Yes, sir, a man named Brodermen. His first name might have been Alfred."

"No, Alfred was his twin brother. Peter was our assistant professor. They both did graduate work here in anthropology. I knew Peter quite well. What specifically would you like to know about him?"

"He had a rather heated public debate in the press with Dr. Stelgis Kara-Kash. I've heard it cost him the Nobel."

"Yes, I remember."

"Why did Peter Brodermen leave here?"

"He left shortly after that unfortunate public dispute. He was never really happy here. He lost interest in anthropology when he was turned down for an appointment at the American Museum of Natural History. I've heard that Dr. Kara-Kash, one of their trustees, was responsible. It explained some of the things that happened later. He was, as I said, only an assistant professor. We asked for his resignation and he tendered it, even though he had tenure."

"Do you know the circumstances, Mr. Sterling?"

"Yes, I was a member of our ethics committee at the time."

"Could you tell me what led to your action?"

"I could, but—well, I don't want to do anything that would hurt him in his present position."

"You can be certain, sir, that I wouldn't use any information you might give me to his disadvantage."

"All right, I believe you. I never liked Brodermen—he was a know-it-all with no sense of tact, a womanizer and —well—I hope he's learned his lesson." When I didn't speak, he continued. "Actually, the incident that cost him his position here involved Dr. Kara-Kash's daughter. She wasn't quite seventeen, I believe. Came from New York to ask him to stop attacking her father in the press, and said he was terminally ill and he might be up for the Nobel again. She met him at his apartment, and accused him of trying to rape her."

"Did he?"

"He denied it, of course, but one of your doctors came down here and accused him to his face before our committee, saying that the girl was underage, that she had had severe emotional problems and was in therapy because of the trauma."

"Was it Dr. Theodore Semminetti?" I asked.

"Yes, that was his name. He was a very angry man, very emotional. He said he would file criminal charges if he had to. I believe he would have if we had not acted to avoid bad public relations for the university. I had a long talk with Brodermen after he resigned. He admitted that he had tried to make love to the girl, but that she went to pieces and scared the hell out of him. I believed him, but I was glad to see him go."

"Do you know where he is now, sir?"

"He went with IBM, I heard, in their sales department. Has an executive position now, in Armonk, in Westchester County."

"Thank you, Mr. Sterling, for being so co-operative," I said. "I won't take any more of your time."

I thought of Sophia throughout the two-hour trip back to the city. One more piece had fallen into place: the emotional breakdown that Dr. Karsloff and Dr. Semminetti had each mentioned was now explained. I could imagine that this unfortunate experience had only added to psychological problems; it explained her fear of men, her reluctance to be touched. What a waste.

When I reached Penn Station, I took a cab and on impulse gave him the address on Central Park West. The night doorman was at his desk. When I asked if Dr. Kara-Kash and her son were in, he said, "Yeah, Joe told me they got back around five this afternoon."

He took my name, then picked up his phone. "There's a Dr. Golm here to see Stelgis, Dr. Kara-Kash," he said. "I'll tell him."

I waited at the elevator. When the door opened, Stelgis

stepped out and ran toward me. "Hey, Gus, I called you the minute we got here. Yong Ha said you were in Philadelphia. Come on up."

I followed him into the elevator and we went up to the fifth floor. The door was ajar and Stelgis escorted me in.

Sophia Kara-Kash stood in front of the grand piano in the large, beautifully furnished living room, her eyes questioning as they met mine.

"I should have called first," I said, "but I was wondering if I might take you both to dinner."

I watched the color rise in her cheeks. "Thank you very much, Dr. Golm," she said, "but we're very tired after our trip. I—we're waiting for a caller."

"It was just an idea," I said. "I'll be on my way. How about a ball game one day this week, Stelgis? I'm on vacation. The Yankees are playing Boston on Friday. Think you can make it?"

"Sure, Gus. And I want to go when the White Sox come to town. Yong Ha said you'd get his thing on Friday."

"That's right. Well, I'll call you."

She remained standing, watching me, no expression whatever on her face, then said, "I'm sorry, Dr. Golm. I should have offered you a drink."

"No, thanks. I'll be in touch."

I met Dr. Semminetti coming from his apartment, just before reaching the elevator. He was without his coat and I was sure he was on his way to the Kara-Kash apartment. For a moment, I could see his real feelings in his eyes; then he gained control of his emotions.

"May I ask what you are doing here, Golm?"

"I was on my way from Penn Station and decided to stop off and say hello to Stelgis."

"You just won't accept advice, will you? I understand you were in Philadelphia today."

"That's right. Went down to look at a psychiatric newsletter they're putting out at the—"

"I know that."

I heard the elevator coming up. As it stopped, I turned to him and said, "You were right about Brodermen. His name is Peter. Has a brother named Alfred. I met a guy down there who knew him well. He works for IBM now, in Westchester."

The same hateful expression came to his face as he turned away and went toward the Kara-Kash apartment. I entered the elevator and went down to the lobby. Lieutenant MacMann was getting out of a cab in front of the building. He recognized me and came forward, his hand outstretched. I motioned for the cab to wait.

"They got in from Chicago this afternoon," I said. "Please be gentle with her, Lieutenant."

"Oh, I will. I just want to ask the boy a few questions. I'm really here to see Dr. Semminetti. Do you think he might be home?"

"Yes, I think he's with the Kara-Kashes. How's your investigation coming along?"

"Well, we keep plugging away. I'll be seeing you, Doctor."

"Good night."

There was a heavy cloud bank rising over the Palisades as I walked up to the tower and I felt sure that a break in our beautiful weather was coming.

Yong Ha was just going on duty when I entered the building. He handed me an envelope containing the paper from the *Illinois State Medical Journal* and told me he had talked with Stelgis. He went back to his studying as I entered the elevator.

I put Brahms's "Concerto in D" on my stereo and sat down to read the paper. It was a preliminary report on an ongoing study. She wrote concisely, without embellishments; it was an interesting and unusual study.

She had acquired eighteen three-day-old rhesus monkeys from a breeding farm in Florida, separating them into three groups of six. Each group was placed in an identical environment, protected in air-conditioned cages with one-way mirrors. The first group was placed in the cages with their natural mothers. The second group was alone, but they were taken out by humans for feeding and fondling several times a day. The third group was left alone constantly and was fed entirely by mechanical hands manipulated from outside, having no contact with humans or other monkeys. At the end of six weeks, the monkeys in the first two groups were slower in their development than monkeys in a normal environment, but were normal in every way. The third group was quite different: they had withdrawn from each other, remaining in fetal positions unless disturbed for feeding, giving every appearance of autistic, schizophrenic children. However, on the fourth and fifth months, one of the small monkeys in the totally isolated group began to show a radical change in behavior. This monkey had a white marking on its head. An investigation by the veterinarian chief of the Department of Comparative Medicine, revealed that an elderly Negro man, who worked nights on the floor, admitted that he had felt sorry for the animals and had removed the monkey with the distinctive marking to play with it. Various biochemical blood studies were being carried out on all of the animals, which would reveal marked differences in the blood factors of each group.

Thinking of Sophia as I went to bed and waited for sleep, I knew that there could be no doubts about her brilliance and abilities as a scientist. I understood, with her shyness and fear of emotional relationships, why she would find teaching threatening and difficult and would want to give all her time to research. I knew that she could be helped, but I was equally certain that therapy could be successful only if she were removed from Dr. Semminetti's influence. Whatever his feelings for her might be, I was convinced that he would continue to try to keep her dependent upon him. How could I possibly get Sophia or Dr. Semminetti to accept this? The decision, of course, would have to be made by Sophia. Could I possibly make her understand how important such a decision might be? It would have to be approached through her concern for her son; perhaps I could win her trust through this indirect advantage, which I now had. Of one thing I was absolutely sure: I could never use the information I'd learned about her and her son; she would have to reveal it to me, in her own time and way.

Just as I was dropping off to sleep, the telephone rang. It was Dr. Karsloff.

"How'd you make out in Philadelphia?" he asked.

"I had a nice visit with Dr. Pollatan. I went through their first seven issues and quite a bit of their correspondence. I think we can do it better."

"One of your virtues, Golm, has never been modesty, but I agree. I want our publication to be a model for other states to follow. It will influence our future grant money. How do you propose setting this project up?"

"I thought, sir, that after I spend three or four days with my parents, that I would try a dummy of the first issue. I have several ideas. How much can we spend for printing and—"

"Whatever amount you feel is necessary. You might contact the hospital's information office. I'd forget your visit to Indiana for the time being. Suppose we have a look at your copy and layout for the first issue by next Wednesday?"

"But, sir, that's not nearly enough time. I'll need at least a four-pager, but eight pages would be better."

"All right, in that case I'll expect it on Monday week."

"But that means I get no vacation at all."

"Yes, it's a hardship, but we all have to make sacrifices. By the way, Dr. Semminetti came in to see me when he returned from Chicago. He's demanding now that I remove you from involvement with Sophia and the boy."

"What was your decision, sir? I hope—"

"I told him to keep his nose out of things that I've arranged. He left in a huff with his feathers up again. Level with me, Golm, what do you feel about that relationship now?"

"I think he keeps her dependent on him, but that she's quite capable of straightening out her life, if left on her own."

"That's what I think. She wants to come back, but only as a researcher. They want her at the college. I've been thinking I might get Semminetti a year's sabbatical in Europe. Of course, it probably couldn't be arranged until September, maybe later."

"Will he do it, sir?"

"I may be able to convince him it's in his best interest if he wants a full professorship. If I have to, I might even throw in an endowed chair. Keep me informed of your progress with the newsletter."

Without saying so, I knew that he was pleased with me, that perhaps the things Dr. Donaldson had told me in Hanover were true.

Chapter Twelve

There was a violent electrical storm at 4 A.M., awakening me in time to close my window. It was still raining when I went down to the hospital cafeteria for breakfast. I met Charley Helms there. He was being called back to Emergency Service for the day.

"How's your plan working out?" he asked.

"I don't feel too good about it, Charley. I think we should call it off. I have a new assignment, which I can't talk about now, but I won't be seeing Dr. Falstein anymore."

"My God, Gus, have you had a change of heart, just when it's started to work? Maybe you *can't* call it off."

"What do you mean?"

"Margaret is throwing a special party tomorrow evening. I'm even invited, so is Falstein. Did you get an invite?"

"Yes. And I'm going to go. Where the hell is the hospital's Office of Public Information?"

"On the first floor, opposite the patient information booth. "What's up, my friend?"

"I can't tell you yet. See you at the party."

I left him and went down the corridor and entered the Office of Public Information. The director, a garrulous old man, about ready to retire, told me much more than I wanted to know about his problems—printing and the constant battle with the college and the hospital administrators. I was grateful, though, when he called the James A. Waters Printing Company downtown on Church Street and set up an appointment for me. He also gave me a couple of dummy forms. I thanked him and returned through the tunnel system to the tower to keep out of the rain. My appointment with the printer wasn't until three, so I worked on a rough layout.

It stopped raining shortly after lunch, so I went out to the subway with my briefcase. The A train took me to within a block of the printer's plant, on the eigth floor of a building that had probably been old when the Flatiron Building was constructed. I took the tiny elevator, which wheezed asthmatically up its worn guide rails, entering an old-fashioned front office that had four roll-up desks and a bull pen, where three clerks and a switchboard operator were busy. James A. Walters, Jr., rose from the first desk and came forward, admitting me through the swing gate. He was in his early fifties, a personable, outgoing but nononsense man who probably had an ulcer. I had a feeling that he knew his business and wouldn't take advantage of my ignorance.

I gave him a summary of my project, said that I wasn't sure of the print run we'd need, but that I thought it would probably be a minimum of the thousand copies. I showed him my rough layout, apologizing for it, saying that I'd appreciate his suggestions for a design for the masthead, a rendered dummy along the lines I'd indicated and an estimate of the printing costs based on a six-month and a yearly contract.

He said, "You seem to know what you're talking about, Doctor. Where'd you learn about printing?"

"I had a year in an ad agency. Did mostly copywriting, but sometimes had a small hand in production."

He accompanied me to the elevator, offering to buy me a drink, but I refused; I already knew that we would get along well together.

I returned to my apartment, changed clothes and went to work. I would use actual case histories of two or three cases with which I had been involved at the hospital's specialty units—an anorectic girl at Children's Hospital who used food to manipulate her family and doctor, losing dangerous amounts of weight almost at will . . . a case of school phobia, seen so often in the outpatient clinic, and by family doctors ... a typical older surgical patient who became amnesiac when awakening at night, frightened and out of contact, wandering from bed to fall down a stairwell. I would pull their medical records tomorrow. I finished about seven, surprised that so much time had passed. The telephone rang as I was making myself a sandwich. It was Stelgis.

"Are you going to get Yong Ha's prosthesis tomorrow, Gus?" he asked.

"They promised it for tomorrow morning," I said. "But we'll have to postpone the ball game. I have too much to do here."

"Can I come up tomorrow and see you and Yong?" he asked.

"Sure, Stelgis," I said. "Can I talk to your mother? Do you think she'll mind if you come?"

"She isn't here now—she's at the supermarket. I'll ask her when she comes in."

"I can't have you without her permission. And I don't want you slipping out, or telling fibs. Understand?"

"Okay, Gus."

"How are things going?"

"Sophia and Uncle Ted had another argument, but—"

"You can tell me about it when I see you. I've got to hang up now. Have your mother call me, please."

"I'll try," he said, and I knew he was displeased with me.

I finished my sandwich and was having a glass of beer, listening to the news, when Sophia Kara-Kash called back.

"Stelgis told me you want him to come tomorrow and help you with your friend. I hope he's not becoming a nuisance."

"I'll be working here in my apartment," I said. "I'm very fond of him and I promised him I'd let him help, but only if you approved. I'll be with him all the time he's here. Have you thought about the suggestions I made?"

"Yes. I—we've discussed it."

"I'll be working all Saturday, but do you think we might take a drive out to Jones Beach on Sunday? It's supposed to be hot by then."

"I may be busy. I don't want to put you out. You've done enough for us and—"

"When you know me better, Doctor, you'll learn that I never do things that I don't like to do. Think about it. Have Stelgis come to my apartment. I'll wait here for him in the morning. Should he take the subway?"

"I'll drop him off."

She hung up before I could continue. I had a feeling she'd turn down my invitation to the beach.

Margaret Bochmeir called me from Riverdale at nine, trying to sound casual. "Just wanted to check—to see if you'll be coming to dinner tomorrow evening. Mamma needs to know."

"I probably won't be able to make it," I said. "I'd like to, but Dr. Karsloff has given me a big job, with very little time to get it done. I'll probably have to work the entire weekend. Better just give me a rain check."

"Oh, I'm sorry," she said, "but I understand."

I was damned sure she was relieved.

I went to bed early, reading a novel I picked up at the patient's library. It was a beautifully written story and seemed appropriate to my mood. It was Graham Green's *End of the Affair*.

I didn't waken until almost nine on Friday morning. I got up and showered quickly and was barely dressed when my buzzer sounded. Stelgis stood there grinning at me, wearing new slacks and a new sports jacket. When I commented on them, he said, "She got me some new clothes yesterday. I didn't want to wear this today, but she made me. Getting hot outside. Can I take my coat off?"

"Of course. It's nice to see you, pal. Been to the museum since you got back?"

"Nah, I promised her I'd stay away from there this summer. She told me about you asking us to Jones Beach."

"Do you think she'll go?"

"She doesn't like to go to beaches, but I'm working on it. I think I know how to bring her around."

"I'm sure you do. What do you have in mind?"

"All I got to do is work it so Uncle Ted forbids her to go. That's what happened before."

"When?"

"When she told him last Monday that she was going to have dinner with you. He said absolutely not, so she went. Uncle Ted doesn't think much of you, Gus. He doesn't think much of me anymore either."

"Why do you say that?"

"Can't you guess?"

"I suspect he isn't pleased that you were in his apartment, going through his files and taking things."

"Yeah. I don't think Tony Peroni gave him back that case history."

"No? I was almost certain he did."

"I asked him about the boy Joe said had visited him. He said it was the son of one of his women patients who had promised him to write something he'd asked for. He says he has them write things they're too embarrassed to tell him. There's no folder back in the 'K's,' that's for sure. I looked again after he left early this morning."

"Didn't he want to know what you'd done with his papers?"

"I told him I'd burned them."

"Why would you say a thing like that?"

"He knows why. I told him I didn't like what he'd written about me and Sophia."

"You did read it then?"

"Just some of it. She had bad dreams the night we flew back to Chicago. She said something about you, but I couldn't make out what it was."

"How is everything else going?"

"Oh, we had a detective visit us right after you left the other evening. Uncle Ted was there and wanted to stay, but Lieutenant MacMann said he wanted to talk to me alone."

"I hope you co-operated with him. He came to see me, too. I think he's a pretty nice guy."

"He told me he'd talked with you. He just wanted me to tell him if I'd seen anyone else around while I was waiting for Tony. He asked me some questions about that cab driver who took off with my money—he got me my money back. I just told him what I told you. What about Yong's thing?"

"I talked to the instrument shop. Mr. Jensen told me I could pick it up anytime." We walked down to the institute to get it and listened to its creator tell us how to use it.

"It's not very effective," he said. "Actually, I put most of this together for old Dr. Morris, who had a patient who got the hiccups when he became upset and couldn't stop. It worked, but I think it was mostly the conditioning—as long as he thought he was going to get a shock, he didn't get hiccups. I made you up a little remote control. When you press the button within five or six feet, he'll get his shock. If you do it a few times, it'll make him think the next time."

He held the apparatus for us to inspect. "As you can see, the straps are adjustable. The large one goes around his waist and has the electrode on the inner side, which is placed on his bare skin. It also has the pocket for the energy cell, which you plug into the sphygmomanometer. It responds only to the systolic pressure. I'd place it around his upper leg as tightly as possible. It shouldn't show under his clothes."

"Thank you, Mr. Jensen, youv'e done a fine job. How much do I owe you?"

"Oh, bring me a bottle of good wine when you think of it. I've had the damned thing lying around since Dr. Morris left. Be interested to know how it works out for your patient."

"We'll let you know."

Stelgis looked up at me when we were out on the street, heading back to the tower. We both grinned, thinking of the same thing. He suddenly put his hand in mine. I knew that in a very short time I had won his trust, but I was sure that he wasn't yet ready to tell me why he was so sure his father had been an Ice Age man.

Yong Ha was just getting up when we knocked on his door. He was in a foul mood, as usual after sleep, and knew exactly why we were there. Like a patient arriving at the dentist's office, he no longer felt a need for our prosthesis. "We'll be back in ten minutes. You take your shower, okay?" He continued to scowl until we left.

When we were in my apartment, I placed the apparatus on the table, handing the remote-control box to

Stelgis. "Step back a few feet and press the button when I put my hand on the electrode," I said.

My hand was on the copper electrode as I looked away from him for a moment. He laughed as my hand shot upward, then hit the button a second time as my hand again made the contact. I bit the end of my tongue, and could still feel the numbness vibrating in my finger.

"It sure works, Gus. Do you think it's too strong?"

"No, it's about right. Let's go."

When we entered the apartment, Yong was standing in his shorts, his body already tense. "Maybe we won't need shock, Glom. I stop and think now. Maybe now—"

"Stop that nonsense! You've been after me all week. Now this little air cuff goes right around here. I pump it up like this—is that too tight?"

He screamed. "You shock me."

"It's not even connected, for godsake! Now stand still. When it's tight as you can stand it, you buckle this belt to keep it in place, then you remove this little pump by unscrewing it. The valve will hold the pressure. Now we'll hook this other belt around your waist and buckle it in front. There, that's it," I said, plugging the power cell into the leg apparatus. "All set. Go in and put your clothes on and let's see if it shows."

He ran into the bathroom, slamming the door. I felt for the remote-control box in my pocket, careful not to activate it by accident. When he came out a few minutes later, fully dressed, no one could have known that he was wearing the instrument.

"It's great," I said. "You must wear it every day when you go to class or are working in the X-ray suite. I'll have to tell Dr. Vandermeer about it."

"No chicken—"

I pressed the button at the moment his neck began to swell. He screamed as he shot into the air like a Russian ballet dancer. I held him tightly until he relaxed. "Easy, just take it easy. See, it *works*. Now just remember that you'll get that juice every time you lose your temper. It wasn't too bad, was it?"

"Okay, Glom. I glad you not put it lower. It was one by god big surprise. You not tell Vandlemeer?"

"Not if you don't want me to. I *am* concerned about something he told me about you, though."

"What Vandlemeer say, that—"

"That he was told you tried to put your hand under that little Filipino girl's dress—the one who works in—"

"Vandlemeer mother-flucking liar. I never—"

I held him again until he calmed down. "I just made that up to see how you'd react. It works, and it'll work every time you explode like that. I want you to keep thinking about it."

"Okay we take it off for a while, Glom?"

"Not on your life. You've got to get used to wearing it. When do you go on duty?"

"Not till noon. I skip class this morning. You think shock not go off by accident?"

"I'm certain it won't, but you'd better think before you blow your stack next time. If your leg starts going to sleep, just let a little of the air out by pressing the valve stem where the pump screws on. You can pump it up later. How about giving Stelgis a tour through the big X-ray suite?"

"Okay, Glom. You come with me, kid."

Stelgis looked at me and winked. "Let me get my jacket first," he said. He followed me to my apartment.

I gave him the remote-control box, warning him not to use it unless Yong Ha should have an explosion. He promised.

I followed them to the elevator. "When is your mother coming to pick you up, Stelgis?" I asked.

"She said four-thirty. If you asked her, maybe I could stay all night and we could—"

"I don't think we should press our luck. Besides, I've got to work."

I was still smiling, remembering the expression on Yong Ha's face as he received his second shock.

They returned just before noon. Yong Ha left for duty, and I took Stelgis to the cafeteria for lunch. On the way down he said, "I only had to use the remote control once, Gus. When we were crossing the street to the hospital a cab came around the corner fast and almost hit us. He started exploding, then he let out that yell and jumped into the air again. But it's going to work. I know it is."

"Why do you say that?"

"I think they tease him a lot—those guys working in the X-ray rooms. One of them snuck up behind him. He jumped, started to explode, then he stopped to think. He just turned around, looked at the guy and said, 'You do that again, I'll knock your bridgework out, Kantrowitz!' "

"That's wonderful!"

After lunch, I showed him through the new emergency room, then took him up to the records department, where I had them pull the ones I needed. He was interested in the new computer system that could tell where every medical chart was at any given time. His questions were always intelligent and he was curious about everything. When I asked him, on our way back to the tower, if he'd thought much about what he wanted to be when he grew up, he said, "I guess I want to become a doctor."

"That's great, Stelgis. I think you'll be a good one."

He stayed with me in my apartment throughout the afternoon, reading my last copy of the A.M.A. journal, watching me write, but didn't interrupt me. At four-thirty, we went down to wait for his mother. She was turning into the drive in a sleek little BMW as we came outside.

Stelgis ran forward to open the door. "It worked, Sophia. It really worked! You should have seen Yong's face when he got his first shock." He was a little boy again, anxious to tell her about all the new things he'd seen.

I closed the door after he got in, then leaned down. She was wearing white slacks and a turtleneck sweater. I kept my eyes on her face, watching her search for words as the color rose in her cheeks.

"We've had a nice day," I said. "I hope we can go to the beach Sunday."

"Please, Sophia—"

"I doubt that we'll be able to make it," she said, "but thank you for asking us—and for having Stelgis today. We really must get home now."

I watched them go down the drive and turn at the corner, feeling frustrated and helpless, like I'd felt in the eighth grade when I'd wanted to kiss Grace Hunter but didn't know how to go about it.

I returned to my apartment and wrote steadily until almost midnight, finishing the report on the anorectic girl and half of the report on the amnesiac elderly patient. I was going to enjoy this part of my new assignment.

I was in my pajamas when my door buzzer sounded. Charley Helms, half-stoned, grinned at me when I opened the door.

"You're not going to believe it," he said, as he followed me into the room, flopped down in a chair and asked for a drink. "Some party. Some house. You must be out of your mind, turning a setup like that over to Falstein."

"He was there then?"

"He sure as hell was. I've never seen such steaks, and the apple strudel was the best I've ever tasted. Our dear preceptor sat there, like a damned dummy. Have you seen that music room? Old Oscar got out his violin, Bertha went to the piano, Margaret brought out her cello and a viola, then an extra music stand. I'll say this for him, he can certainly play the damned thing, and none of them could believe he hadn't practiced with them before. The four of them were still at it when the rest of us left. Jesus, Gus, did you know that old Oscar owns twenty-three delicatessens and that Margaret is their only child?"

"Yep, I believe I heard him say something about it once."

"You're crazy to give that up. How about another drink, old buddy?"

"It's time to go, Charley. You have early duty and I have a big day tomorrow."

When I finally got him out, I went to bed. I tried to read Graham Greene, but my mind was on Margaret and Dr. Falstein. I felt now no sense of loss whatever at the news Charley had brought me; instead, I felt very pleased with myself. They made a perfect couple. In my own good time, I would convey my congratulations to both of them, wish them well and really mean it.

Chapter Thirteen

I rose early Saturday and continued my writing, finishing the three main features of my first issue. It was almost five when I looked at my clock. I hurried down to the institute, but Dr. Karsloff hadn't been in since noon. His office, however, was open and I left my copy, with a note asking if he could have the typing pool do a final draft after he had corrected it. Then I crossed over to the hospital to return the medical charts. As I passed the information booth, I suddenly remembered something and asked the clerk if a package had been left for Dr. Golm. He handed me a blue envelope. I went to the large leather sofa across from the booth and opened the package, feeling pleased and surprised at the fine job that Waters's designer had done. She had managed to use my long title—*Emotional Problems in General Practice*—so that it fit the masthead well. The layout was clean and attractive, with almost perfect hand-lettering for heads and subheads. Just as I was going toward the door a cab stopped outside and the director of Public Information got out.

"Hey, what are you doing in here on Saturday?" I asked him as he came through the door, keys in hand.

"It always happens on a weekend," he said. "I got a call to come in and help a family with an obit—old Dr. Phillip Snyder. Used to be chief of the Obs-Gyn Service. His daughter and son-in-law are meeting me here."

For a moment I was too stunned to speak. "I—I can't believe it," I said. "I spent the afternoon with him only last—we had lunch. Do you know the circumstances?"

"No, I just got a call from the present chief of Obs-

131

Gyn to come in and help with the obit for tomorrow's *Times*. . . . That must be them now." He went out to greet them.

I recognized the daughter as she came through the door and stepped forward to meet her. "I'm Dr. Golm," I said. "I was with Dr. Snyder at your house."

"Yes, of course. We—we're so upset. I blame myself. I've been busy at our church's rummage sale all week and I had to leave him alone." She began to cry.

I took her hands, squeezed them, then turned to her husband, a handsome, reserved man. I introduced myself, then asked about the circumstances of death.

"He was in the sun porch. He must have fallen striking his head on the corner of a table. The doctor's certain that he then had a heart attack. He's had two small attacks during the past two years. He was almost eighty-four, you know."

"Will there be an autopsy, sir?"

"Oh, no!" he said. "Our family doctor doesn't feel it's necessary. I wouldn't want to put my wife through that."

"I understand."

Death is a constant fact of life in any physician's daily routine, but this one had struck me with unusual impact. I remembered his interest in my patients and their problems and I thought he had seemed in unusually good health for his age. I was still thinking about him as I walked back to the institute. Then, out of the blue, I remembered that I'd told Dr. Semminetti that I was planning to talk to him about Stelgis's birth. It was too fantastic to take seriously, but after feeling this strange man's anger, I knew that he could very well be capable of murder. I continued to think about it after I reached my apartment, trying to put the terrible thought from my mind, but it wouldn't go away. On impulse, I decided to call Dr. Semminetti and confront him with the news of Dr. Snyder's death. If I caught him by surprise, he might reveal something that would either confirm or erase my suspicion. His number was still on my desk pad. I dialed it, let the phone ring several times, finally hanging up.

I was about to dial Sophia when my phone rang, causing me to jump. It was Stelgis.

"Hey, I was about to call you, pal. You scared me."

He laughed. "Has Yong Ha had any more explosions?"

"I haven't seen him. I think he's spending today with one of the guys he works with. I just tried to call Dr. Semminetti, but he didn't answer."

"Oh, he left this morning, in one of his bad moods."

"What happened?"

"Sophia told him you'd invited us to go to Jones Beach. He was really upset this time, Gus. Told her she absolutely couldn't go. That's all it took. What time do you want us to pick you up in the morning?"

"Hey, that's great. Let's go early, before the good spots are all taken. How about ten? There's a good deli up here on Broadway. They make great picnic baskets. I'll—"

"Naw, Sophia is fixing a basket. She's got two barbecued chickens and a lot of other stuff. We used to go out to the beach on the south shore of Lake Michigan. She doesn't swim much, but she likes to sunbathe. It's going to be a scorcher."

"Do you know where Dr. Semminetti went, Stelgis?"

"Sure. He said he was going to drive up to Boston for the weekend. Do you think Yong Ha could go with us tomorrow?"

I thought about it for a moment, then said, "No, I don't think so. He's off, but he'll probably still be with his friend in Rockland County. See you at ten." I hung up, sure that I'd made the right decision. Introducing a stranger into our beach party could only inhibit a person as shy as Sophia.

I continued to think about her as I mixed myself a drink. It was now obvious that she was striving to develop independence and break the hold that Dr. Semminetti had on her. I felt grateful that he'd been so injudicious as to forbid her to go out with me a second time. I fixed myself a bacon and egg sandwich and fresh coffee, then returned to my writing.

Yong Ha rang my buzzer shortly before ten and came in beaming, patting the instrument on his leg, his face sunburnt.

"Prosthesis work okay, Glom. I know she's gonna work now. I think all the time about that juice hitting me."

"Where the hell have you been all day?"

"I go home with Kantrowitz. We go to Lake Welch in Bear Mountain Park. Sun hotter than by god. I hungry."

"Go ahead, pal. There's bacon and eggs and some Sara Lee cake in the freezer."

Yong ate his supper and watched television while I worked until almost eleven, then said good night.

"What time do they bring the papers in down at the desk?" I asked.

"Early, Glom. Sometimes before seven. Why?"

"One of our old doctors died early this afternoon. They were writing an obit for the *Times'* early edition."

"I get it for you in morning. I got early duty in out-patient clinic at eight. I take Kantrowitz' place."

My buzzer sounded promptly at seven on Sunday morning. Yong Ha handed me the paper, then said he had to run.

I turned to the obits in the second section. Dr. Snyder's picture, undoubtedly taken several years ago, was given two columns, followed by a list of accomplishments throughout a distinguished career. There would be private funeral services in Englewood for the family only, and a memorial service at the medical center chapel on Tuesday.

As I started to lay out shorts and a shirt to wear to the beach, it occurred to me that my swimsuit was still in the Bochmeir bathhouse. I called Margaret at Hadley Hall, but got no answer, then tried her home. She was still sleeping and had to be called.

"Hi, Gus," she said. "What are you doing up so early?"

"I'm going with my young patient and his mother to Jones Beach at ten," I said. "And I just remembered that my swimsuit is at your bathhouse. I guess I'll have to take a cab over and pick it up."

"That won't be necessary, Gus. Daddy has to go to the airport and pick up my aunt at nine. I'll have him drop it off at the tower desk. It's not much out of his way."

"Sorry I missed your party. Charley Helms said there was some great music."

"Yes, we had a great time. Have a nice day at the beach."

Her voice was distant and cold, and I knew that I would never be invited to Riverdale again.

Chapter Fourteen

I was standing on the sidewalk in front of the tower as they turned into the circle, holding my old airlines bag, which contained two beach towels and my swimsuit. Stelgis was wearing his swimsuit, shorts and sneakers. I could see that Sophia was also wearing her swimsuit under her slacks and shirt. When I opened the door and started to get in beside Stelgis, she said, "Would you mind driving, Doctor? I'm not sure of the road out there and the traffic is certain to be heavy on a day like this."

I hurried around the car to open the door for her, then went back to open the other door. As we turned uptown toward Harlem River Drive, she said, "I think we should plan to start back early. I hope you don't mind driving. I just didn't know the way."

"I don't mind at all—especially with a beautiful little car like this. We used to go out there often last summer."

As we crossed Triboro Bridge and drove east on Grand Central Parkway, I thought of old Dr. Snyder again, but decided to postpone mentioning his death. She continued to look away from me, glad, I was sure, that Stelgis continued to chatter, relieving her of the need to make conversation.

I continued to steal glances at her from the corner of my eye, until she caught me at it. The color rose in her cheeks as she turned away. I made no effort to engage her in conversation, but continued to talk to Stelgis, telling him about my new project. I knew that she was interested, even though she continued to look away from me. She turned suddenly, smiled for the first time, and said,

135

"Stelgis knows about school phobia, Doctor. Don't you, Stelgis?"

He grinned sheepishly, looked at his mother, then said, "I missed school four days in a row before she found out from the teacher. He thought we'd gone out of town."

"What did you do during all that time?"

"Oh, I went down to the Loop on the I.C., saw a lot of movies, ate a lot of hamburgers, walked out on Navy Pier and watched a lot of old men fishing."

"Why didn't you want to go to school?"

"Oh, you know—I told you about it."

"I don't remember that you told me about missing school."

"It was when the kids started calling me those names."

I saw the expression on his mother's face change, and she interrupted him before he could explain further.

"Stelgis, I want you to promise me now that you'll behave yourself when we get to the beach. None of your tricks."

He looked up at me and grinned.

"What kind of tricks, pal?" When he didn't answer, I turned to his mother.

"He goes out into very deep water beyond the markers, then pretends he's in trouble."

"You'd better not do anything like that today," I said. "There's a good breeze and the waves will be high and there may be an undertow."

"I'm a good swimmer," he said.

We crossed over the causeway just before eleven, parking in the third lot. I opened the trunk and removed a styrofoam cooler and a picnic basket. We crossed the white sand to a relatively empty spot, stopping forty yards from where the white-capped waves were roaring in.

"If you two will spread the blanket and towels, I'll go over to the bathhouse, put on my swimsuit and pick up a couple of umbrellas."

When I returned fifteen minutes later, she was lying in her swimsuit staring up at the cloudless sky through her sunglasses. She appeared even smaller without her street clothing. I stopped behind her. When I spoke, she was startled and rose up quickly, pulling one of the towels across the front of her body.

136

"Where's Stelgis?" I asked, as I implanted the handles of the umbrellas in the sand.

"He couldn't wait," she said.

I turned away from her and walked toward the water, where a lifeguard sat in his tower. Stelgis was almost out to the marker buoys. He saw me, waved, then began to swim toward me. "Come on in, Gus. The water's super."

I hesitated, then ran out to meet a large wave, dove through it, floated up and over the next one, then swam to Stelgis, who was grinning and treading water. I could just touch bottom with my toes. He splashed me and I went after him. We swam for several minutes, riding the large waves into the beach.

"I've had enough for a while," I said, "but don't let me spoil your fun."

Two other boys his age came into the water. He joined them and waved at me as they swam toward the marker line. When I reached our umbrellas, Sophia was still lying with the large towel across her body. I flopped down beside her, but continued to look out toward Stelgis and his companions.

"Wouldn't you like to go in for a dip before it gets crowded?" I asked. "It seems awfully cold at first, but it's really warm today."

"Perhaps later," she said. "There's beer in the cooler, a bottle of gin and some tonic water. Would you like to mix us a drink?"

"Sure. That's a fine idea"

When I handed her one of the glasses, I met her eyes and smiled. She hesitated, but returned my smile.

"It's such a lovely day," she said. "I—I'm glad we came. Aren't the gulls beautiful, and those little long-leg brown birds—what kind are they?"

I followed her eyes, watching the graceful gulls as they rode the air currents, gliding up and down, watching for food scraps. Then I noticed the little long-legged birds running in and out with the receding waves, picking sand crabs and other tiny sea creatures from the wet sand.

"I don't know much about seabirds," I said, "but I would suspect that they're sandpipers. They look a bit like the snipe we used to hunt in Indiana when they came north in the spring."

"Did you like to kill things, Dr. Golm?"

"I did when I was Stelgis's age. All boys are natural hunters. I shot my last quail when I was home from medical school at Christmas during my first year. I haven't hunted since."

"I'm glad," she said, not looking at me. "I can hardly bear it when one of our research animals must be sacrificed. Someone else has to do it for me."

"I know the feeling."

She took another large swallow of her drink, continuing to watch the birds, then said, "I've been thinking about what you recommended for Stelgis. I know you're right, but it will be so difficult to be separated from him."

"Of course it will."

"He talks of you constantly—you and Yong Ha, Dr. Golm."

I waited a moment, then said, "Why don't you just call me Gus, because I'm going to call you Sophia? All right?"

She continued to look at me through her sunglasses, her beautiful face impassive. Without seeing her eyes, I couldn't determine whether my suggestion had been accepted or rejected. When she continued to be silent, turning back to watch the birds as they ran with waves, I said, "I still have eight days of vacation time. If I can finish the first issue of my newsletter in time, could we drive with Stelgis to visit a very good school I've heard about in Connecticut? It's just below Hartford."

"Uncle Ted—Dr. Semminetti—is recommending a school in New Hampshire. He wants to drive us up there next weekend. I think he might be offended if we went with you.

"Has he—have you discussed it with Stelgis?"

"No, not yet. I've been avoiding it."

"Why?"

"Stelgis has become very negative with Uncle Ted."

"Yes, I gathered as much. Do you know why?"

"Uncle Ted has been—well, rather harsh on him recently."

"What would you like for Stelgis, Sophia? I mean when he grows up. It's understandable if you haven't thought that far ahead, but—"

I jumped as a glob of wet sand struck my bare back,

followed by another that landed on Sophia. A loud laugh came from behind us. Stelgis stood there, hands on hips. "Come on in, you two. The water's great."

"Stelgis, that wasn't nice at all," his mother said.

I turned slowly about to face the water, waiting. Another handful of dry sand sprayed my back. I rose slowly. "You are not to do that again, Stelgis," I said quietly.

He met my eyes, his expression changing, then bent down to pick up sand in both hands. I continued to stare at him, waiting. He suddenly threw the sand and it struck me in the face. As I stepped toward him, he turned and run toward the water, stopping at its edge. I walked slowly toward him. He must have read my intentions, because he ran into the water, dove through the breaking wave and began swimming toward deep water. I followed him, catching him when we were about fifty yards from the beach. I enfolded him in my arms as he squirmed and tried to break loose. I swam with him until my feet touched bottom, then carried him through the breakers. He began to struggle as I propelled him toward his mother. When we stopped in front of her, his slippery body turned in my arms and he struck me on the side of my face with his clenched fist. I shook him, then slapped him with my own open hand. He stared into my face, wilting suddenly, tears in his eyes.

"You are not ever to do that again, Stelgis," I said, keeping anger out of my voice. "Now apologize to your mother." His expression remained sullen as I continued to look at him, waiting. "All right then, you can sit over here by yourself until you're ready to apologize." I picked up one of the towels and moved it a few yards to our right, then moved one of the umbrellas to shelter it. He continued to stand there, scowling, looking from his mother to me. I went to him, took him by the arms and propelled him to the towel. When he refused to sit down, I tripped him, forcing him down, then sat down beside him, feeling sorry for him as I watched his lips tremble and the tears that suddenly spilled out and ran down his cheeks.

"I want to be your friend, Stelgis," I said, "but what you did was rude, thoughtless and inexcusable. Now sit here until you are ready to apologize."

He suddenly turned over on his stomach, burying his

face in his hands, kicking his toes in and out of the sand. I watched him for a few moments, then rose and went back to Sophia, dropping down on the towels beside her. She was wearing an expression almost like her son's. When she started to rise and go to him, I reached out and grasped her arm. She flinched, but I continued to hold her.

"Wait, please," I said. "This is an important moment for Stelgis—for each of us. Trust me, and just talk normally."

She looked up at me, then relaxed, tears forming in her eyes.

"I read your preliminary report on your research project with the infant monkeys. It was very interesting. Have you found differentiating blood factors among the three groups?" Lowering my voice, I said, "Just talk naturally. Please. He'll be all right in a few minutes."

She hesitated, then said, "We've found variables in the muscular development of each group, in tactile reaction times, mood variables, but serum differentials are difficult to evaluate. They can change from day to day, for various reasons. We have found, I believe, confirmation of the relationship between the biogenic amines and mood. This is not anything new."

"I presume you refer to the induced depressive states in test animals and the resulting depletion in the brain of serotonin, norepinephrine and a number of other amines."

She stole a quick glance at her son, then looked at me. "Yes. A model for research purposes of what appears to be an accurate equivalent of pathological depression can be induced with excessive doses of reserpine, but no such model exists for schizophrenia. I sometimes think that no such model will ever be found."

"I know what you mean, but we shouldn't think it's an impossible search—please, Sophia, trust me. Don't go to him now." She relaxed and lay back down. I continued to hold her arm for a moment, then removed my hand.

I sat up slowly and glanced over my shoulder at Stelgis. He was sitting with his back toward us, staring up the beach, his posture rigid.

"Please come with me, Sophia. It's critical to my future relationship with Stelgis."

I took both of her hands in mine and pulled her to her feet. She was reluctant at first, glancing back at her son, then let me lead her by one hand toward the water. I didn't allow her to stop when she held back at the edge, but pulled her after me through the first breaker, then into the next. We fell forward into the deeper water. I released her hand and she began to swim. I followed her, catching her arm and holding her. My feet were on the bottom and the water came to my shoulders. I held her afloat for a moment, then moved backward until her feet could touch bottom.

"He's watching us," I said, "and he doesn't quite know what to make of us." My arm slipped around her shoulders and I squeezed her gently, then released her. She smiled suddenly as she looked upward into my face.

"Look, he's coming to join us."

She followed my eyes. Stelgis came into the water, hesitated, then dove through the first big wave and began swimming to meet us as we moved slowly toward him. He stopped a few feet away, his feet barely touching bottom. "I'm sorry," he said.

"I'm sorry, too, Stelgis. Come here."

He swam to us. We each held out a hand, and pulled him between us. His mother gave him a kiss on his cheek, and I ducked his head gently under the water, then released him.

"Come on, I'll race you both in. I'm hungry. Let's eat."

Stelgis was opening the picnic basket as I got his umbrella and towel and brought them back to their original positions. Sophia was on her knees, spreading a tablecloth over the towels, then she removed a platter of sandwiches, deviled eggs, a plate of barbecued chicken, ripe tomatoes and celery sticks spread with cheese. I opened a bottle of Coke for Stelgis and a can of beer for myself and looked at Sophia, smiling. "That's a beautiful picnic spread," I said. "What will you have to drink, Sophia?"

"A Coke, please."

Stelgis remained on his knees beside the empty basket for a moment, then moved over to sit between us. He gulped a tiny ham sandwich, then reached for another. He continued to look at his mother, wearing a perplexed expression that I had not seen before. When his mother

141

looked up suddenly, meeting his eyes, he said, "You went in the water. What happened? You never go in."

She looked at me, blushed, then turned away. "I've been thinking about going in for a long time. Don't eat so fast."

We ate most of the food, then lay back to watch the gulls circling above us, diving for the scraps that Stelgis began throwing out to them. The crowd had started to fill the beach for several hundred yards on either side of us. The boys who had been with Stelgis came toward us, carrying a small surfboard, and asked Stelgis if he would like to try it.

"Sure," he said, jumping to his feet quickly. He stopped suddenly and turned about to face us, looking from his mother to me. "It's all right, isn't it?"

"Maybe you should wait a while after eating?" his mother said.

"No, that's an old wives' tale. Have fun, pal."

We watched him for several minutes, remaining silent, as he tried the surfboard. I reached over and gently took her hand in mine. She resisted for just a moment, then relaxed, but didn't look at me.

"I'm very fond of Stelgis, Sophia," I said. "I know how sensitive you are, how difficult it is for you to—to be natural with me. I would never do anything to hurt either of you. You were about to tell me something when Stelgis threw the sand. What do you really want for him when he grows up? He told me that he guessed he wanted to become a doctor."

She sat up, gently removing her hand from mine. "I find it difficult to—to feel relaxed with people, not just with you, Gus. I missed so many things growing up as a child."

"Yes, I suspected as much. You'll overcome those feelings. I'd like to help you."

She smiled suddenly. "I—I would like very much for Stelgis to grow up and have your confidence, your way of making others feel at ease. We have so many problems, Stelgis and I."

"None of them are insurmountable. I've had my problems, too, but I believe—"

"Oh, God, no!" she cried, a look of horror on her face.

I turned quickly to follow her eyes. Three large gulls were screaming and diving toward one of the sandpipers that was fluttering along the wet sand, apparently struck by the beak of a gull. It recovered, beginning to hop about in circles, until struck again. The gulls landed on the sand, then began tearing it apart with their beaks and talons. The feathers continued to rise as the gulls fought over their prey. One gull finally grasped what was left of the little bird's carcass in its talons and flew away, chased by the others.

"Oh, God, oh—"

I reached for her, and she came into my arms, sobbing as her body trembled against mine. I began to talk softly to her, rocking her gently like a small child. I had never before in my life felt so gentle, so filled with love.

"Hey, what's going on with you two?"

I released her and she rolled away from me to bury her face in her hands. I rose quickly and went to Stelgis, taking his hand, leading him back toward where the little bird had been killed, explaining gently to him what had happened.

"It was a terrible shock to her," I said. "We'll leave her alone until she recovers. Do you want to go in again?"

"No," he replied. "We should take her home. She doesn't get over things easy."

When he removed his hand from mine, I knew that he, too, was undergoing something strange and frightening. It would take time for him to share his mother with anyone else.

"Okay," I said. "Will you help me carry the umbrellas back to the concession stand?"

"No. I'll stay with her."

She was still lying on her stomach when we reached her. I carried the umbrellas and my clothes toward the bathhouse, stopping at the concessionaire's booth. I showered then returned to Stelgis and his mother. They had folded the blanket and towels, repacked the basket and were waiting for me.

Sophia had put on her slacks and shirt over her suit and rose from the sand as I approached, her features still set in the same frightened mold. "I'm sorry, Dr. Golm," she said. "I'll be all right now."

We were silent as we drove to New York. Stelgis had his hand in Sophia's, and didn't look at me or speak. When I tried to make conversation, he said, "I don't want to talk now."

"I understand," I said. And I knew there was another facet in the boy's relationship with his mother that I hadn't suspected before.

It was almost four when I stopped in front of the tower. I got out quickly with my bag and held the door for Sophia. "I think I've fallen in love with you," I said softly. "Things will work out for us. I won't rush you."

She didn't speak, but got in when I opened the door. "Good-bye, Stelgis," I said. "I'll call you tomorrow." He didn't reply. I watched them until they disappeared around the corner.

No one was at the desk when I went inside, but the day clerk had left a pink telephone slip for me on the spindle. Lieutenant MacMann had called at two o'clock, asking me to call him when I returned.

I went up to my apartment and called him.

"This is Dr. Golm, Lieutenant. I just got in."

"Thanks for calling back, Doctor. I need very much to talk with you. If you have plans for this evening, I could come up first thing in the morning."

"No, I'm free for the rest of the day. Come to my apartment in Butler Tower, four blocks north of the institute. It's fourteen-o-five."

"Good. I'll be there within the hour."

I mixed myself a scotch and soda, turned on the tube and sat down to wait, thinking of the expression on Sophia's face as she watched the bird die. The severity of her reaction could be due only to one thing—she was seeing the tiny bird as herself, torn to pieces, unable to reconcile the forces that were clawing at her; Stelgis and his special needs, Dr. Semminetti, who was demanding more than she wanted to give, me and my overt intrusion into her life. I thought of my final words to her, wishing that I could recall them until she was better prepared for such a threatening new challenge.

Chapter Fifteen

As I finished my drink and mixed a second, I felt my anxiety turn to anger as I watched "Movie for a Sunday Afternoon," which was interrupted every few minutes. I watched and listened to intelligent and undoubtedly moral men and women sell products that were not only ineffective but potentially dangerous. A serious, deep-voiced man, wearing a white coat and looking more like a responsible physician than old Dr. Snyder, extolled the therapeutic values of an over-the-counter drug that could induce relaxation and sleep; he did not mention that its active ingredient was an antihistamine that could be dangerous if taken in large doses. Another, equally convincing, made his pitch for a nostrum with extra-strength ingredients for people suffering the pain of arthritis; he did not say that it was mostly common aspirin that could be purchased for half the price.

I turned the set off, feeling exactly like that man in Nevada who had used both barrels of his shotgun to blow out the picture tube.

My buzzer sounded, and I opened the door, admitting Lieutenant MacMann, who carried a brown envelope.

"Sorry to bother you, Doctor, but—"

"It's quite all right, Lieutenant. What's on your mind?"

"Well, I got a call from Dr. Donaldson up at Hanover State. It seems that the Kara-Kash boy had an envelope when he went into that meat locker. It apparently was under that box they found him on and wasn't found until they moved it yesterday. Barkus didn't know what to do with it, so he took it to Dr. Donaldson, who called me. I went up and got it yesterday afternoon."

"What did the envelope contain, Lieutenant?"

"Some very strange papers."

"Were they in a folder—a doctor's case-history folder?"

"No, Doctor. There were two medical reports from an institute in Russia. I got the translations this morning. They just don't make any sense to me. There were also two letters in English—very bad English—and copies of the replies. I thought you might be able to help me make some sense of this."

"Do you have them with you?" I asked, looking at the envelope in his hand.

"No. This is something I have to drop off at the Thirty-fourth Precinct Station. But I can tell you about them. My inspector has the material locked in his safe."

"I wish you'd brought them for me to read."

"I wanted to, but the inspector wouldn't turn them over to me. I guess he's had some bad experiences with doctors and medical centers."

"How?"

"When one of their people get in trouble—well, they try to protect them. At least some of them do."

"The letters, I presume, concern one of our doctors."

"Yes, the Kara-Kash boy's grandfather."

"I see. Tell me about them."

"It's really crazy, but after Dr. Donaldson told me about the boy's statement about his father being an Ice Age man—well, maybe they do make sense."

"Tell me about the Russian scientific reports first."

"They say that following an atomic test in northern Siberia, a huge glacial disturbance occurred more than eighty miles away. Half of an ice mountain split apart, and they found underneath a perfectly preserved Ice Age man, who apparently had been frozen almost instantly, approximately eighteen thousand years ago. They had sectioned this victim's testes and found live human sperm. Sounds fantastic, doesn't it."

"It certainly does."

"But three eminent Russian scientists, according to the report, had examined the corpse and the sperm and declared it a responsible report. We checked them out. Two of them are still living and are active in research in Russia today."

"I—I can't believe it. There has to be some explanation other than—"

"That's what we think. The second report is actually a confidential memorandum from the Russian institute to the Russian secret police. It states that one of their scientists—a Dr. Yura Asinoff—disappeared from the institute, taking the specimen of frozen sperm from the Ice Age man."

My reaction must have shown in my face, because he said, "You look like you might have an idea of where this frozen sperm might have ended up, Doctor."

"No, it—it just seems too fantastic to accept as authentic."

"That's what we think, and our sources in Washington think so too. This material is from the middle sixties when we first began to have scientific exchanges with the Russians. Our State Department believes that the Russians might have faked this whole thing in order to make one of our great scientists appear foolish, especially if he were a candidate for the Nobel Prize."

"You mean Dr. Kara-Kash?"

"Yes. The first letter I mentioned was from London, sent by Dr. Asinoff to Dr. Kara-Kash. It said that he defected from Russia to England and had valuable scientific secrets. He said he was coming to America and would like to meet with Dr. Kara-Kash, asking him to name a place and time. Dr. Kara-Kash replied that he would meet him wherever and whenever it could be arranged after he arrived in New York. The second letter was from New York, but gave no address. It simply confirmed a date and asked that Dr. Kara-Kash bring five thousand dollars in cash. Dr. Kara-Kash acknowledged this letter also, agreeing to the cash request, but there was no address given."

"Have you talked with anyone else about this?" I asked.

"Yes, I tried to talk to Dr. Semminetti the other evening—but that was before I had this information. I just wanted him to tell me if he knew why the Kara-Kash boy could have developed his strange ideas about his father."

"Did he have any explanations?"

"No. He gave me a lot of double-talk about the kid being a borderline mental case, and insisted that I not question either the boy or his mother, saying that it would be dangerous to their mental health."

"Are you going to tell her what you learned from the Russian papers?"

"That's why I came to you, Doctor. The boy seems okay, but I believe the mother could be close to a mental breakdown, like he said. Do you think I should talk to her?"

"I hope you won't. I agree with Dr. Semminetti about her mental condition. I do think you might talk to Semminetti again though. He was very close to old Dr. Kara-Kash in those days, and he might be able to give you more information. You can be sure that he won't reveal anything to the boy's mother."

"I'm glad to hear that. I've been trying to reach Dr. Semminetti by phone since yesterday afternoon, but get no answer. Do you think I'll be able to reach him here in the morning?"

"I'm sure he's supposed to be on duty in the afternoon. I heard that he went to Boston for the weekend. Could I get you a drink, Lieutenant?"

"Thanks a lot, Doctor, but I have to go up to the Thirty-fourth and then meet my wife for dinner Midtown. Thanks for your help."

I freshened up my drink and returned to my chair, my head spinning from the things the lieutenant had told me. Whatever risk there might be of further worsening my relationship with Stelgis, I knew the time had come when I had to question him.

I went to the phone and dialed their number. Stelgis answered.

"I hope your mother's feeling better, Stelgis," I said. "Do you think I might talk to her?"

"I'll see." There was a wait, then he came back to

the phone. "She can't talk now," he said. "She took a sleeping pill. I—I'm sorry, Gus."

"About what?"

"You know—how I acted at the beach and not saying good-bye to you. I don't like to see her—"

"I know exactly how you feel." I glanced at my watch. It was six-thirty. "If I came down in a cab, could you meet me at the corner of Seventy-seventh at the park entrance? We could take a walk down to the zoo."

"Sure. She'll be asleep until midnight, at least."

"Good, I'll meet you there in half an hour."

He was waiting for me on the corner when I got out of the cab, running to meet me, taking my hand. I felt tremendous relief that his hostility had disappeared. I put my arm around his shoulder as we entered Central Park and walked downtown toward the zoo.

"Stelgis, I'm going to be honest with you, and I want you to be completely honest with me. You haven't in the past, I know that." He looked up at me, color rising in his cheeks. "I think I'm in love with Sophia. I want to marry her, if she's willing, after she gets to know me better. I think we might build a good life together. What do you think of that?"

He didn't speak, but his hand tightened in mine. We walked silently for some time, then he said, "I'm afraid, Gus."

"Of me?"

"Oh, no! If—could we live in Indiana? I mean if—"

"Would you like that?"

"Oh, yes—with the river and lakes and—and kids like you grew up with."

"Then what are you afraid of?"

"Uncle Ted. I heard him talking to her, just before he left for Boston. They didn't know I was in the bedroom. He wants to take Sophia with him."

"To where?"

"Italy. He said he's got a chance at an appointment there in a university medical school. He wants to put me in a school in New Hampshire. He—he wants Sophia to marry him. Oh, Gus—" He stopped and started to cry.

I put my arm about his shoulders, drew him to me, holding him close, then released him, holding only his

149

hand. We walked a while before he recovered and said, "I didn't know he felt that way about her, honest I didn't, Gus."

"Well, she's a beautiful woman and he's a lonely man, very much in love with her, I'm sure. It would depend on how she feels about him."

"But she doesn't even like to be around him. That's why we stay in Chicago. When he found out she was thinking of coming to the medical center here, he began to act and talk crazy. I'm afraid of him, Gus, and she's afraid of him."

"Hey, don't be frightened, Stelgis. We'll work it out. I'll see that he doesn't harm either of you. Would you like a hot dog?"

"Sure. There's a cart up on the street."

We went to the edge of the park and bought hot dogs and soda from the vendor, then walked down to the zoo to look at the animals. We started back toward Seventy-seventh Street, stopping at a bench that was near the park entrance.

When we were seated, I said, "Stelgis, you haven't been honest with me about what you took from your Uncle Ted's files."

"Yes I was, Gus."

"Now stop it! Lieutenant MacMann has the envelope you left under the packing box in that meat room in Hanover. It contained some documents you took from his files."

"But I didn't get them from Uncle Ted."

"Where did you get them?"

"I found then in one of grandfather's trunks—that Saturday and Sunday when I came to New York."

"What made you look there?"

"She caught me going through it last summer, and told me I wasn't ever to open it again. She must have told Uncle Ted about it, because he took it from our storage locker and put it in the closet in his apartment."

"Why did you take the papers to camp? The truth, now."

"I told you—I wanted to make copies of them, and the other stuff."

"Did you?"

"Yes, in the library at Hanover."

"What did you do with the copies?"

"I hid them under my cabin floor. I was going to take all the stuff back and put it where I'd found it—all of the originals."

"How many copies did you make?"

"Two—that's all I needed. There's a place down on Forty-second Street, near the library, that will translate any language. I was going to leave one copy with them and keep one for myself. That's why I wanted to come to New York on a weekday. I was going to slip back out of that—that Barkus place before they opened next morning, but I went to sleep. What—what do you think that cop will do with the papers?"

"I'm not sure, but I know he won't do anything to hurt you or Sophia. Did you have those papers you took from Dr. Semminetti in that envelope with the Russian things?"

"Sure. I told Uncle Ted I burned them, but he's not sure that I did."

"Why do you say that?"

"He keeps asking me about it, and he says he doesn't believe me."

"You've fibbed to him before?"

He grinned, nodding his head.

"Now for the big one. I need to know: do you have any idea at all of what was in those Russian papers and what Uncle Ted wrote in Italian?"

"No, but I can guess. I wanted to get translations to be sure."

"Tell me what you think is in them."

"I think they tell how I happened to be born and who my father was."

"Thank you for being honest with me, Stelgis. I'll never doubt your word again. You'd better get back to Sophia. Maybe she'll let you come up for the day on Wednesday."

He took my hand again as we walked out of the park and up Central Park West toward their apartment building. I was shaking his hand at the door, my other hand on his shoulder, as I said good-bye. A cab pulled up to the curb as he entered the building and I turned around, raising my hand to the cabbie. Dr. Semminetti got out of it, his face livid with rage as he approached me.

He stopped in front of me, his mustache twitching, his eyes malevolent as they met mine.

"I've asked you for the last time to keep away from this place, Golm. Get out of my way!"

I stepped aside. He passed me, stumbling over the small step, then disappeared into the building. I went out to the cab and gave him my address at the tower.

Chapter Sixteen

I woke early Monday morning and went down to the institute to have breakfast. Dr. Karsloff was there, at his usual table, with his coffee and doughnut. When he nodded, I joined him. He looked at my eggs, bacon, hashed-brown potatoes and oatmeal, covered with cream, shaking his head, the same look of disgust in his eyes.

"And you don't seem to gain a damned pound," he said. "What's this crap about crediting the medical center with our publication?"

"After reading the letters Dr. Pollatan received and thinking of my father's reaction to anything relating to psychiatry, I believe family practitioners, surgeons and even internists can be turned off just by seeing the word 'psychiatry.' "

"But what will the National Institute people think? Their grant money is given to promote psychiatry in general medicine."

"Maybe if we wrote them, giving our reasons, they might go along with us."

"You feel that strongly about it?"

"Yes, sir, I do."

"I'll see what they say."

"What did you think of the layout and my copy?"

"They'll do, but I rewrote some of your copy on anorexia nervosa. You left out a point that general phy-

153

sicians should know, even though it wasn't important in this case. One of the steps a doctor should take is to avoid appearing too concerned with the patient's weight. I had a case, the wife of a top Wall Street broker, who hated her husband. She accumulated four refrigerators full of meat scraps, food she'd brought home from restaurants. Hoarding food, as you know, is a common symptom. But this woman trained as a dietitian, knew to the calorie how much and what to eat to protect her health, even when she dropped from a hundred twelve pounds to only eighty pounds. She was just a bag of bones, but she was healthy as a horse. The husband was mad about her, had her in and out of private sanitariums, before finally coming to me. I wouldn't touch the case until he agreed to commit her. We tube-fed her for a week, but she regurgitated it later and her weight remained constant at eighty pounds. One day, when we were having our session, I forgot to weigh her. She went into a tirade, demanding to be weighed. That's when it struck me. I told her that she would not be weighed again, that she would goddamn well eat or starve to death." He smiled, remembering.

"Did she start eating?"

"You're damned right she did, after four days. Was up to a hundred and ten when I discharged her."

"Did you see her again?"

"Yeah, ten years later. She weighed a hundred and eighty, was healthy as a horse, concerned only for her husband, who was admitted as an alcoholic."

"Have you any ideas that I might use for future cases, sir? You've probably had more tough cases that you've successfully treated than any other psychiatrist in America."

"Stop the bullshit, Golm! I'd like to see you use the juvenile diabetic who manipulated and punished her parents, her doctor, her teachers and, later, the young guy she married. Once they learn they can do it, they'll almost kill themselves to have their way. I've seen them go into hyperglycemic shock, even when they know it's going to happen."

"I suppose they simply skip their insulin?"

"That's right. And some of them substitute sterile water. It can be dangerous, and g.p.'s should always suspect it when they can't seem to adjust insulin dosages. I'd like to see a case of myxedema. It's often mistaken for depression and withdrawal. We've had a dozen cases that needed only thyroid shots to control it. You might do a straight piece on the symptomology of early schizophrenia. The same on potential suicides. I'll have some medical charts pulled for you. How're you making out with Sophia?"

I told him about our trip to the beach and her reaction to the death of the bird, and the manner in which I'd handled Stelgis's tantrum. He listened, nodding his head approvingly.

"Poor thing," he said. "You'd better be careful, Golm, she may not be ready for someone like you."

I looked down at my food, then said, "I wouldn't for the world do anything to hurt her."

"It's gone that far, has it? Watch yourself, you're vulnerable."

"In what way, sir?"

"You've really got a soft streak, you know, but you'll learn. You respond—maybe sometimes overrespond—to your patients' needs. Falstein's noticed it, too. Don't ever lose that feeling for patients, but try to gain insight into your own responses. I've got to go to another damned staff meeting now. Actually, I'm impressed with what you've done so far."

I wanted to tell him about my conversation with Lieutenant MacMann, but he was gone before I could stop him. I'd also wanted to ask him if he'd had anything to do with a possible sabbatical in Italy for Dr. Semminetti. I was sure he'd talked to him about it, but I was just as sure he would resent me questioning him.

I finished breakfast, then went up to the psychiatric library. I came down for lunch, then went over to the Office of Public Information to go through their large collection of photographs.

I met Dr. Vandermeer, who was responsible for radiology services to all clinic outpatients. He stopped me. "Can you tell me, Dr. Golm, what is responsible for the remarkable change in your Korean buddy?"

I thought of my promise to Yong Ha, smiled and said, "As you know, I've been working with him, trying to help him stop and think before he explodes under stress. Do you mean to say you've seen improvements?"

"We have indeed. I've been worried about him—all of us over there have. I know his background, but we also place our reputation on the line when we send the wrong kind of technician out with our certificate. The boys over there tell me he now seems in control. They deliberately try to set him off, but he hasn't been responding since late last week. I want to congratulate you."

I went to my apartment at four and took a nap, waking shortly after six when Yong Ha buzzed my door.

"You want to go down to Canton Restaurant, Golm? I work overtime, miss the cafeteria, I hungry."

"Why not?" I asked. "There's nothing much left in my refrigerator. Wait until I dress. When do you have to go on the desk?"

"Not till nine. Jimmy owe me three hours."

We walked down to the hospital, then went down Broadway to the small Chinese restaurant where Yong Ha always got a warm welcome. When he dropped down on the seat across from me, I heard his leg instrument bump against the seat.

"You're still wearing it, aren't you?"

"All the time now. It works, Golm. I *think* now."

"I know you do, and I'm proud of you. Know what Dr. Vandemeer told me when I met him in the hall this afternoon?"

"What Vandlemeer say?" he asked.

"He said there wasn't any doubt now that you'll get your certificate. He said all of them have tested you and that none of them have been able to trigger your temper."

His face began to glow as the grin spread across it. "He really say that, Golm?"

"Of course he did. I wouldn't lie to you."

"I glad. I write Big Mike."

"Who's Big Mike?"

"My fadder, Sergeant Masters. Everyone call him Big Mike."

"I've wondered about something, Yong. I know Big Mike adopted you. Why haven't you used his name?"

"He not want me to. Say I look like damn fool with name like Masters."

"What's your mother's name?"

"Olga. She one damn fine lady."

"How'd a Chinese girl get a name like that?"

"Her mamma was Norwegian. Her father had one fine restaurant near Schofield Barracks. Big Mike go there often."

We finished eating shortly after eight. The thunderheads that had been rising out of the west throughout the afternoon were coming in fast now, with thunder and lightning flashing across the sky. The wind and rain struck as we ran into the Broadway entrance of the outpatient clinic. Yong Ha stopped as we reached the triage counter. "I got to go upstairs and get book," he said. "You not have to wait."

"I'm going to take the tunnel to the tower," I said. "I'll walk slowly and you can catch me. Maybe we can have another game of backgammon this evening."

"Okay, Glom."

I walked to the front entrance of the hospital, saw that it was still pouring, then went back down to the tunnel. I walked slowly under the large steam and water pipes, feeling the heat and humidity, passing the side tunnels that led to Hadley Hall, Hadley Pavilion and the Hadley Neurological Institute. I turned north when the tunnel divided, one going to the School of Nursing, the other toward the Psychiatric Institute and Butler Tower. I could hear steps in the tunnel I had just left and knew by the sound that it was Yong Ha trying to catch up with me. I slowed down but continued, wanting to get out of the heat. As I passed the entrance tunnel to the institute I noticed that the light was out above the junction. I'd taken only a few steps when I froze, every nerve in my body responding.

"Watch out, Glom!"

I whirled about to my right, striking my head against the wall of the narrow tunnel. I heard something strike the wall, bounce off and up the terra-cotta flooring. As I rose and turned about, Yong Ha was running toward me.

"That somnoblitch going to jump you, Glom!"

"Who?"

"I not see good. He run back in institute tunnel."

I hurried back to the tunnel junction, but the tunnel to

the institute was clear. I suddenly remembered the sound of something striking the wall. We walked back and found the dart lying under the light, twenty yards from where it had been deflected. I picked it up carefully and examined it. It had been whittled out of very hard wood, then scraped smooth around its cylindrical surface. Two feathers protruded from its back end and the front end had been beveled down to a long slender point, which had broken when it struck the concrete wall, but was still hanging by a slender strand of wood. The first inch of the point had been grooved with a sharp object around its entire surface and coated with a black resinous substance. I wet my finger, touched the substance, then tasted it. It was very bitter. I knew that it was an alkaloid, probably curare. Had it struck my back instead of the wall, it would have imbedded itself in my flesh, my motor nerves would now be paralyzed and I would be feeling the first symptons of suffocation. I realized that I had missed death by inches.

"I go find somnoblitch, Glom! I know he go into tunnel."

"Don't you remember anything at all about what he looked like?"

"It dark. I too surprised when that shock hit. It really work, Glom."

"And I'm lucky it did. Come on."

I wrapped the dart in my handkerchief, holding it carefully, as we hurried up the tunnel, which had two exits. We stopped at the first stairwell, which led up to the receiving dock of the service building. When we reached the door, it was still slightly ajar. The loading platform was empty and there were no trucks or cars or on the vehicle area or on the street in front of it. We crossed to the institute. The security guard was sitting at his desk near the front entrance, reading. The tunnel door opened a few yards to his right.

"Hi, Martin," I said. "Has anyone entered here within the last ten minutes, or come up from the tunnel?"

"No, Dr. Golm. Real quiet night."

"Any of the attendings upstairs?"

"Are you kidding? Just the house staff."

"Thank you, Martin."

We went outside. I looked across at the lighted loading platform and the vacant spaces along the street. Whoever it had been had probably gotten out through that exit to the street.

"Come on, Yong, I've got some calls to make."

We hurried to my apartment. I went to the phone and dialed Dr. Semminetti's home number. I let it ring for a long time, then finally hung up and dialed the Kara-Kash number. There was a long wait before the phone was picked up. There was a pause, then Sophia answered in a low, hesitant voice: "Yes."

"This is Gus, Sophia. May I speak with Stelgis?"

"He isn't here, Doctor."

"Where is he?"

"I've been sleeping. He said he was going to a movie with his friend. Is—is anything wrong? You sound so—so different."

"No, everything is fine. I just wanted to talk to him about coming up Tuesday. I'll call him in the morning. Sorry to have wakened you. Good night."

I put the phone down, thought for a moment, then found Lieutenant MacMann's card in my desk drawer and dialed his home number. His wife answered. She said that she was expecting him home any minute. I gave her my number and asked that he call me the moment he got in.

I went back to the living room and picked up my handkerchief and the dart. I felt revulsion as I looked at the deadly, primitive weapon.

Yong Ha was looking at his watch when I glanced up at him.

"I got half hour, Glom. You want to play backgammon?"

"Not tonight, Yong. Thank you for yelling in the tunnel. I think you saved my life."

His eyes were startled and his lips puckered as the reality of what had happened struck him for the first time.

"You mean somnoblitch try to kill you?"

"That's right, but don't say a word to anyone about it. Okay?"

"Okay, Glom. I go down now and let Jimmy go home early."

I mixed myself a stiff drink after he had gone and sat

in my big chair. I thought of Stelgis, the expression on his face when he struck me, the way he had reacted when he had found his mother in my arms, his anger as we drove home from the beach. I was also remembering the things Dr. Semminetti had told me about him—that he couldn't experience normal emotions, that he reacted impulsively and was becoming harder to control as he matured. Had I been wrong in my judgment of him? The phone rang and I jumped, hurrying to answer it.

"Good evening, Dr. Golm," Dr. Semminetti said, his voice calm and professional. "I've just returned from my office. Sophia is very upset. We were wondering if Stelgis might have come to your apartment. He left his mother around six, saying he was going to a movie with a boy in our building, but the boy said he hadn't seen him."

"He hasn't been here, Doctor. I talked to his mother only fifteen minutes ago."

"I know. We just wanted to be sure he hadn't been there. Call us at once if you hear from him. Dr. Kara-Kash is terribly worried and upset. Sorry to have bothered you."

I put the phone down and returned to my chair, feeling even more confused. The telephone rang again. It was Lieutenant MacMann.

"Good evening, Dr. Golm. My wife said you wanted me to—"

"Yes, Lieutenant. Could you come up to my apartment immediately? It's very important. I'm sorry to bother you at this time of night, but—"

"Forget it. I'll be there in twenty minutes."

I sat down to wait. It seemed hours before my buzzer sounded, but it had only been twenty-five minutes. My telephone rang again as I was admitting the lieutenant. I asked him to sit down and went to answer it. It was Stelgis.

"Hi, Gus. Sophia said I should call you."

"Where the hell have you been all evening?"

"To a movie—that one with Jane Fonda, *Coming Home*. She's angry at me, said I couldn't come up on Tuesday."

"Did you go with your friend?"

"Naw, I just told her that, so she'd let me out. Maybe she'll let me come up Wednesday?"

"Okay, let me know. Good night."

I returned to Lieutenant MacMann. Stelgis was either the most dangerous psychopath I had known, or as innocent as I had imagined.

"Can I mix you a drink, Lieutenant?"

"That sounds good. I've had one hell'va day. A little scotch on the rocks, with a dash of bitters if you have it."

I fixed his drink and took it over to him where he was sitting on the sofa, then sat in the chair across from him.

"To your good health, Doctor."

"That's an appropriate toast," I said. "I'm beginning to think my health is in jeopardy."

I watched his face as he sipped his drink. He appeared relaxed, making no effort to rush me toward an explanation. He was a good cop, experienced and sure of himself. When I remained silent, he said, "You sounded upset on the phone."

"Yes, and I had good reason to be. What do you think about this little present that was almost delivered in my back about an hour ago?"

I picked up my handkerchief and unwrapped the dart, handing it to him. He took it carefully in both hands, stared down at it under the lamp, then looked up to meet my eyes.

"It's curare, I'm sure. It's harmless unless it breaks the skin."

"You've seen something like it before, you said."

"Yes. I think you should tell me what happened, Doctor."

I gave him a detailed account; he was shaking his head as I finished.

"I don't believe you've been completely frank with me, Doctor—about the boy and his mother. I sensed when I talked with you the other morning that you were holding back. After this, don't you think you should tell me everything you know about this child?"

"I had a feeling that you were also holding back information, Lieutenant. This child is my patient. I have professional responsibilities and——"

"Yes, I know. We both have responsibilities. I'll be as

161

frank as I can. This dart is a mate to the one that killed the Peroni boy, but they're not the darts that were stolen from the museum." He noted my surprise, continuing when I did not speak: "We have the three darts that were taken from the museum. I found them among the Peroni boy's things."

"Where could these darts have come from?"

"We don't know for sure, but they have many types of poisonous arrows and darts locked away at the museum. They could have come from there, if one had access to them, and your patient apparently did. What's your opinion of Dr. Semminetti?"

"What's yours, Lieutenant?"

He smiled. "Let's stop fencing, Doctor. I know you have professional responsibilities, but we're dealing with murder and a very dangerous murderer, as you damned well should know after this evening. I'm going to level with you, but you mustn't reveal the things I'm going to tell you. I won't use anything you tell me in a way that might embarrass you or this medical center. Agreed?"

"Yes. Let me freshen your drink." I got the bottle and poured two fingers of scotch over his ice.

"I believe Dr. Semminetti is a very disturbed, potentially dangerous man. I've suspected that he might have killed the Peroni boy, especially after you told me you felt Stelgis hadn't done it. He—"

"Go on, Doctor."

"After tonight, I'm not so sure. I believe the boy may be a psychopathic personality. He's precocious and brilliant, as you know, secretive and cunning, and is capable of doing anything he sets out to do. The true psychopathic personality acts on impulse. His mood can change from affection to anger at the slightest provocation."

"Yes, that's the same picture Dr. Semminetti gave me. He said that Stelgis gave a boy in his class in Chicago a terrible beating, and that he tried to drown the Peroni kid at camp. What do make of his delusions, or whatever you call them, about his father?"

"Until tonight, I felt that he had a realistic basis for his beliefs."

"Go on, please. Explain your reasons."

I felt the last of my resistance go. I told him all I'd

learned about Stelgis and Sophia—about the clippings, and the information about Brodermen and his attempt to rape Sophia. I hesitated, then finally told him what I'd learned about the frozen sperm.

"So that explains the secrets the grandfather paid five thousand dollars to get. Is it really possible, Doctor, that this sperm came from an Ice Age man?"

"I don't know," I said. "I don't believe it could happen, but who knows how long human sperm can remain viable in a frozen state? There are several thousand men in this country who have their sperm in banks, taken before vasectomies were performed. It's a safeguard in case they should want children later."

"Could the boy's mother have impregnated herself with this sperm?"

"Yes, it's a simple procedure. Or she could have had it performed at any one of several fertility clinics in this city."

"Could Dr. Semminetti have performed it?"

"Yes, of course, but I can't see Sophia turning to him."

"I can. In addition to the Russian reports found in the boy's envelope, there was a twenty-two-page handwritten document in Italian. We also have its translation."

I leaned forward, listening, watching his face as he searched for the right words.

"It's a scientific paper. It mentions no names, but refers to the female as 'the subject.' It details the birth of the baby and its development through the fifth year of life. What is the Sheldon morphological scale, Dr. Golm?"

"Sheldon was a great scientist, qualified in medicine, anthropology and psychiatry. He took the anthropometric measurements of several thousand college men, eighty measurements in all, I believe, then separated them into three general types—ectomorphic, mesomorphic and endomorphic. He attributed certain emotional characteristics to each group, and classified the diseases each group was most prone to."

"That explains the drawings that accompanied Dr. Semminetti's paper."

"You're certain, then, that he wrote it?"

"Yes. It's his handwriting. Did you know that he was an anthropology major in college, and spent two vaca-

tions in South America with a group from the American
Museum of Natural History?"

"I knew he's switched from anthropology to medicine,
but I didn't know he'd had field experience in South
America."

"Well, he did, and he's a close friend of several curators at the museum. We've been almost certain that Dr.
Semminetti killed the Peroni boy." When he saw the expression on my face, he explained. "The cab driver I
told you about saw a man of Semminetti's description
came out of the park shortly after he let the Kara-Kash
boy out. He was almost running toward the subway station. That's one of the reasons we believe the boy is innocent. The other reason is that the body was found up on
the side of the hill, fifty yards from where the Kara-Kash
boy was waiting for him. Can you think of any reason
why Semminetti would have wanted to kill the boy?"

I thought for some time, then a logical explanation
occurred to me. "I'm certain the Peroni boy was at Dr.
Semminetti's apartment around noon of the day he was
killed. I believe he delivered a photocopy of the paper
written in Italian. Stelgis told me that he'd made two
copies. Could this boy have sold him the one copy, then
called him later to say he had another for a price?"

"You'd better believe that kid was capable of that kind
of play. You should read the record we have on him.
We—I think Semminetti might have thought the Peroni
boy had the originals not only of the Italian article but
also of the Russian papers. Knowing his feelings toward
the mother and his need to protect his own professional
reputation, wouldn't you be willing to believe he might
have killed to get them?"

"Yes, I do. He's a very strange man." Another possibility popped into my mind. "Dr. Semminetti knew I
was planning to have a talk with Dr. Snyder. Dr. Snyder
died the day after I was with him, supposedly of a fall
and heart attack. I had a feeling when I was with him
that he was in good health for his age. Do you think—"

The lieutenant took a notebook from his inside pocket
and made notes in it, then looked up. "I'll believe anything about a man who has killed once. I'd stake my
reputation that you were supposed to be his next victim.

Watch your step from now on, Doctor. I'm going to keep him under surveillance twenty-four hours a day. I wanted to do it last week."

"Why don't you arrest him, if you're so certain of his guilt?"

"We wouldn't have a prayer of convicting him with what we now have. The cabbie only had a glimpse of him. The court wouldn't give me a search warrant on the evidence we have. But I'm going to get him. I think he's gone completely over the edge. And I hope you'll help us."

"How?" I asked, feeling very vulnerable.

"I want you to become our bait. If he tried to kill you tonight, he'll try again. Not immediately, he's much too smart for that. But if we plan it right, threaten him a little more, he'll come for you. We'll make it easy for him, but you'll be protected every minute. We want to catch him in the act. Are you willing to co-operate?"

"I—I guess I haven't much choice. What do you want me to do?"

"Toward the end of the week, get him alone and tell him you have the originals of all his papers. You got them from Hanover State Hospital where Mr. Barkus took them after finding them in his meat room. Are you following me?"

"I certainly am."

"All right. Do you think it might be worthwhile to ask for an autopsy on Dr. Snyder? The Jersey police co-operate with us; we could get an order."

"I hope you don't have to, Lieutenant. His poor daughter is distraught enough. He was a terrific old man."

"I know. I'll miss his birthday cards. Is there anything else you can tell me—any lead at all—however minor it might seem?"

"There is one thing. I was going to call Brodermen. He's supposed to be working for IBM up in Armonk."

"Why him, Doctor?"

"He has a twin brother in the State Department who is, or was, an attaché in our embassy in Moscow. I thought there might be a connection between the Brodermens and those Russian documents. Peter—the one who was at Pennsylvania—apparently hated old Dr. Kara-

Kash. He had a bitter dispute with him in the press over two or three years. I thought—"

"Yes, indeed, Doctor." He rose from the sofa. "Thank you for your help. Just be careful around the medical center. We'll have him tailed wherever he goes outside of here."

After he had gone, I put on my pajamas and went to bed. The buzzer sounded just as I was drifting off to sleep. It was the lieutenant, wearing a sheepish expression on his face.

"I forgot to take the evidence," he said, going to the end table to pick up the dart. "Please don't tell my inspector. Good night again, Doctor."

Chapter Seventeen

I spent most of Tuesday at the library, checking the literature and faking letters from doctors asking questions about patients with emotional problems, knowing that Dr. Karsloff could get some of our attendings in medicine to sign them. There seemed no other way to set the tone for future issues. I then did abstracts of several research papers.

When I went to the institute's dining room for lunch, I saw Dr. Falstein and Margaret Bochmeir sitting together at a table in the corner. Each of them looked up but quickly returned to their conversation, pretending not to have seen me. Dr. Karsloff came in a short time later, smiled and nodded at me, but joined a group of attendings at the large table near the back window. I finished eating shortly after one, then went over to the Office of Public Information to select photographs for the newsletter. I returned to the library and worked until four, completing most of my first issue, then went back to my apartment. I had been there only a few minutes when Lieutenant MacMann called.

"Hi, Dr. Golm. I tried to reach you this morning."

"I've been working at the library. What's up?"

"I called IBM in Armonk, asking for Peter Brodermen. The operator referred me to their personnel department. Peter Broderman was killed in a hit-and-run accident six years ago. He'd been with IBM for about nine years. What do you make of that?"

"It's frightening," I said. "Did you get any of the details—about the accident, I mean?"

"Yes, I talked to the police in Katonah, where he lived. He was something of a drunk, they told me. Used to go to a bar within walking distance of his apartment. He was stoned the night he was killed—at least that's what the bartender told them. He was struck while crossing the street to his building. It happened around midnight and there were no witnesses. The case is still unsolved. Do you think Brodermen might have been our suspect's first victim?"

"It's logical. I know for sure that he hated Brodermen."

"We checked on the brother in the State Department. His name is Alfred. He's been back in the States for the past five years. He lives in an apartment hotel just across the line in Maryland. We've learned that he's scheduled to go abroad again in two or three weeks— to Mexico this time. They apparently think quite highly of him down there. I have his telephone number."

"Why are you telling me this, Lieutenant?"

"We were wondering if you might go down and have a talk with him."

"About what?"

"Those Russian documents."

"Do you think they might be faked?"

"We know they are. There's no such institute of publication in Russia. We thought he might respond better to you than—well, to me or the police down there. You could approach him as the doctor responsible for the Kara-Kash boy. We've made photocopies of those documents, which you could show to him, saying you got them from your patient. If we confront him with them, he'll clam up, and probably take off for his new assignment. There's no way we can stop him. Can you help us?"

"I'll try. There's no guarantee that he'll tell me anything, but—"

"There's one edge you might want to use."

"What's that?"

"If he had anything to do with forging those documents, he might very well be involved in a conspiracy to defraud."

"I don't understand."

"That five thousand Kara-Kash paid for the frozen sperm. It's well beyond the statute of limitations, and there's not a hell'va lot we can do about it now, but he might not know that. Know what I mean?"

"I think so."

"If he should mention that he's beyond prosecution, you might suggest that the New York police are prepared to turn the information over to the State Department, with a complaint against him as an irresponsible representative of the United States. Of course, I wouldn't want you to take such actions unless you're convinced he knows something."

"I can't see why the police wouldn't be as effective as—"

"Haven't you heard, Doctor? New York City is broke. We're being asked to cut every corner these days. Besides, I think you're a very bright guy, and you'd be a better judge of this man's reaction to what's happening since that frozen sperm came into your medical center. Well, Doctor?"

"All right, but I'll have to get approval from my chief of service. Now, what's Brodermen's telephone number?"

I wrote it down on my pad, then said, "I haven't seen Dr. Semminetti today."

"He hasn't left his apartment. I talked to him this morning."

"Did you learn anything new?"

"No. I just told him we thought the Kara-Kash boy might be implicated in the Peroni murder. He agreed with me—a bit too quickly, I thought. Let me know the moment you get back from Washington."

"I will."

I hung up, then dialed Dr. Karsloff's number. Miss Thomas put me through at once.

"What the hell is it now, Golm?"

"I have most of the first issue done, sir. I'm going to Washington this evening."

"For what?"

"It's personal business. I'll be back tomorrow. I'll leave my copy at the lobby desk, with your name on it."

"All right, Golm, but I hope you're not pulling another fast one." He slammed his phone down hard.

I glanced at my watch. It was a quarter of five. I dialed the number the Lieutenant had given me, getting a secretary. When I told her I wanted to speak with Mr. Alfred Brodermen, she wanted to know who was calling.

"Dr. Golm, of the University Medical Center of Manhattan," I said. "It's a personal matter, but I must speak to him."

"Thank you, Doctor. Will you hold for just a moment?" There were only a few moments of waiting. "This is Brodermen, Dr. Golm. What can I do for you?"

"I'm planning to be in Washington tomorrow. Could you possibly have lunch with me? I could meet you wherever you say."

"What specifically do you want to see me about?"

"It involves one of my patients and, indirectly, your brother Peter."

"Peter is dead, Doctor."

"Yes, I know, but I think you'll be interested in some of the information I have."

"You mean about the accident?"

"In a manner of speaking, yes."

"Let me look at my appointment book." There was a pause, then he said, "I can meet you at eleven-thirty for lunch in the main dining room of the Shoreham Hotel. I have an important meeting at one sharp."

"That will be plenty of time, sir. Thank you for seeing me."

"It's okay, Doctor."

I suddenly felt the emotions that every resident feels when he has a day completely to himself away from the medical center. I called Eastern Airlines and asked about a flight that would get me to Washington by 10:30 A.M. and they suggested the 9:30 shuttle.

Then I had an impulse to call Sophia. Stelgis answered on the first ring.

"Hi, Stelgis," I said. "Could I speak to your mother?"

"She isn't here, Gus. I thought it was her calling. She had an appointment with her lawyer at four o'clock. We're supposed to go out and eat."

"How are things going?"

"Same. I'm trying to get her to go back to Chicago for awhile."

"It's that bad, is it?"

"Yeah. We can't take much more of it. She's told him she's not going to Italy. . . . Here she comes now. I'll ask her if she wants to talk to you." There was a pause and I knew his hand was over the phone. "She says she can't talk now, Gus. There's a cab waiting outside."

"Tell her I'll call her tomorrow evening."

Chapter Eighteen

I arrived at La Guardia shortly before nine, in time to catch the first section of their busiest shuttle flight. The second plane was loading as we pulled out to the runway a few minutes ahead of departure time. I sat next to a prim, grandmotherly woman who was going to Washington to see her new grandson. When she learned that I was a doctor, she spent the rest of our flight telling me about her various symptoms, which included a cataract, suspected adhesions from an old stomach operation, arthritis in her neck and shoulder and unexplained headaches that she'd had for several years. What did I think of a friend's recommendation that she go to a chiropractor who was a real expert on neck pain? I avoided answering that question, but was as gentle with her as I could be. She reminded me a lot of my Aunt Charlotte. I carried her overnight bag into the terminal and went out to the street to catch a cab.

The Shoreham was quite far from the airport, but I arrived there a little before eleven. I bought a newspaper and sat down to wait for Alfred Brodermen. I went to the main dining room at 11:25, asking if Mr. Brodermen had made a reservation. He hadn't, but they told me that he lunched frequently there. I was sipping my martini when he came across the room to my table, and I rose to shake his hand.

He was a tall, slim man, conservatively dressed in a well-cut summer suit. His blue eyes and expression when he grinned at me suggested a good sense of humor. He sat down, looked at my drink, then ordered a white wine and soda, his voice revealing a southern accent.

We opened our conversation with a comment on the good weather, the sad state of affairs in Fun City and the inconveniences of short-distance air travel, when the trip from an airport almost equals flying time. He came to the point quickly.

"I do have an important meeting at one, Doctor. You wished to talk to me about one of your patients."

"Yes, his name is Stelgis Kara-Kash."

He put his drink down and I noticed a slight tic under his right eye. When he waited for me to continue, I said, "You've undoubtedly heard of old Dr. Kara-Kash. He was nominated for the Nobel Prize twice."

"Yes, I remember the name vaguely."

"Let's not fence with each other, Mr. Brodermen. Your brother Peter had a long and bitter fight with Dr. Kara-Kash in both the public and scientific press. It cost him the Nobel."

"I thought he'd died."

"He did, back in 1966. My patient is his grandson. He has serious problems, but is a fine boy, sensitive and precocious. He needs help."

"How can this concern me, Doctor?"

"It concerns your brother," I said. "Does the name Semminetti—Dr. Theodore Semminetti—mean anything to you?"

Again his right cheek twitched, and I was certain the name was familiar.

"I thought you should know, sir, that the New York police have been investigating your brother's death. They now have reason to believe that it was not just another routine hit-and-run accident."

"Come to the point, Doctor."

"They think he might have been murdered."

"Are you serious? Peter had been drinking, was—well, something of a chronic lush during the last three years of his life. I was in Russia at the time. I couldn't be here to help him. We were twins, you know."

"Yes, I know."

"He hated Kara-Kash and Semminetti and he had good reason to."

"Was that why he tried to rape Dr. Kara-Kash's seventeen-year-old- daughter?"

"That was a damned lie! I talked with Pete about it. He took her to lunch and they stopped at his apartment to pick up a book he wanted to give her. He simply tried to kiss her, that was all, but she went to pieces. He got her to her train as soon as he could. It cost him his teaching job at the university."

"Was that why he hated Dr. Kara-Kash?"

"No. It went back much earlier—the year we graduated from the University of North Carolina. We majored in life sciences and settled on anthropology. Pete had one great ambition—to get an appointment at the American Museum of Natural History. He had an opportunity to go on a field trip to South America—a three-year project to study and live with a primitive Indian tribe in Peru. He had met the project director, and was accepted, subject to the approval of the trustees. Dr. Kara-Kash headed the committee for anthropology and archaeology. This man Semminetti was his protégé. He killed Pete's appointment and got it for Semminetti."

"That must have been a great disappointment for him."

"He never got over it. It wrecked his career. He lived for one thing, to pay those two back, but he didn't rape the Kara-Kash girl."

"I believe you. Did you know that he was involved in a conspiracy to fleece old Dr. Kara-Kash out of several thousand dollars?"

His cheek began to twitch again. "That is something I very much doubt. I was in Russia, as I said, and—"

"Can you tell me anything about these documents?" I asked suddenly, removing the Russian reports and correspondence between Dr. Kara-Kash and Dr. Yura Asinoff from my inside coat pocket. He read through the first page of the report, then the correspondence. Color showed in his cheeks and his tic continued.

"Can you tell me what this is all about, Doctor?"

"No, I'd hoped you might tell me. There has been one

murder for certain because of these documents, perhaps two others, and one attempted murder. The New York police now know that these papers were forged—no that's the wrong word. They believe they were created out of whole cloth, in Russia."

"How can they be sure of that?"

"They've analyzed the paper on which the originals were printed. The three Russian scientists used to authenticate this specious report were contacted and they denied making such a report. The police were going to come down and question you; they were prepared to go to your superiors in the State Department if you failed to cooperate. I asked them to let me talk to you first."

I knew that I had taken liberties with the truth, but as his anxiety increased and his fingers holding the papers began to tremble ever so slightly, I knew that I'd reached his most vulnerable spot.

"Just why are you so interested in all this, Doctor?"

"Someone tried to kill me a few evenings ago." I decided to take a chance. "The police know that whoever created these papers is now protected by the statute of limitations. However—" I paused. "However, they feel certain you had a hand in it. And they are prepared to file a complaint against you—question your character and responsibility as a representative of our government. They know that you've recently been upgraded and are scheduled for a new post in Mexico."

"But that's devious and—and—"

"I know it is. That's why I wanted to speak with you first. I've learned most of the facts about that frozen sperm, attributed to an Ice Age man. My patient, Dr. Kara-Kash's grandson, now truly believes that he is a product of that sperm and his future mental health may depend upon his learning the truth. The police will drop the case and remove records from their files if you can explain how these documents came to Dr. Kara-Kash, and why."

He wilted suddenly, all his resistance fading. "Do I have your word, Doctor, that no one will attempt to endanger my career?"

"You do."

The waiter came to our table. Brodermen asked him

to bring a scotch and soda. He looked at my half-empty glass, but I shook my head.

He remained silent until his drink came, then took a large gulp, then another. I felt certain that, like the brother, he had a drinking problem.

"You believe that my brother's death can be traced to these documents," he said, handing them back to me.

"I do. I also believe that given the whole truth, the police will bring his murderer to justice."

"All right, Dr. Golm. I'm placing my career in your hands. I was the liaison between the United States and Russian scientific communities. I had many contacts in various research centers and with members of the Russian press. When I came home on leave, Peter told me about his forced resignation at the university. He wanted revenge. I was much younger then, irresponsibly loyal to Pete. He wrote those reports in English and I took them back to Russia, added the names of responsible scientists in the proper disciplines, then got them printed in Russian. I was involved with one scientist who, with the help of our State Department, defected to America when he was sent to a post in England. I gave him the documents, along with instructions on how to get them into Dr. Kara-Kash's hands. I didn't know that he would ask money for them, but it was logical that he should, I know now—"

"Why do you say that?"

"He was not a genuine defector, but a Russian agent, sent to learn all he could about English and American scientific research."

"Do you think the Russian Government knew what you were planning to do with those documents?"

"I'm sure of it, now. That's why I found it so easy to get their cooperation in printing that material. Had Dr. Kara-Kash taken the bait and used that frozen semen, then received the Nobel Prize—well, the world would have been laughing with the Russians at American science."

"Now for the big one, Mr. Brodermen. Just where did that frozen sperm come from?"

He looked down at his drink, shook it, finished it, then met my eyes, the suggestion of a grin on his face. "It was Peter's," he said. "I carried it all the way back to Moscow in an insulated container packed with dry ice. It remained in a Russian sperm bank until it was turned over to Asinoff on the day he flew to England. It was to be Peter's ultimate revenge against Kara-Kash and his daughter."

I could not speak for a moment. What a horrible despicable thing to have done.

"Is something wrong, Doctor? You look as though you don't believe me."

"I believe you, Mr. Brodermen. Would it interest you to know that you have a nephew, a delightful little boy who is now certain that his father was an Ice Age man?"

"Oh, my God!"

"His name is Stelgis Kara-Kash. Dr. Sophia Kara-Kash, old Dr. Kara-Kash's daughter, inseminated herself with that frozen sperm, or had it done. Could—did your brother know of this?"

"I'm not certain—no that's not true. I'm sure he did know. He wrote me that his trick had worked, better than he ever dreamed."

"Could he have told the child's mother what he'd done?"

"In his frame of mind, he would have been capable of it. No, I take that back—Peter was not really a cruel person. His real hatred was for Dr. Kara-Kash and Semminetti. He might have told Semminetti, if he knew about the child's birth. You say he is a fine boy, the child?"

"Yes, a truly delightful and lovable boy."

"I—wonder if I could see him sometime? Our father and mother died while Pete and I were doing graduate work at Pennsylvania. Peter was all the family I had left. He had substantial insurance and retirement annuities with IBM. I was his beneficiary. He never married." Tears came to his eyes.

I looked at him, truly liking him for the first time. He had participated in a cruel hoax, but I could now understand why.

"Is—do you think there might be a way for me to place the money Peter left in trust for his son?"

"That's a generous thought, but he doesn't really need it. His grandfather left his mother a substantial inheritance. Not immediately, but perhaps in time I could arrange for you to meet your nephew."

"I would like that very much, Doctor." Again tears appeared in his eyes.

We ate our lunch in silence, each of us embarrassed by the information we'd shared. I walked with him out of the hotel to catch a cab. Just as he was entering it, he stopped and turned back to face me. "Do you think Semminetti might have killed my brother?"

"It's a distinct possibility," I said. "I'll keep you informed of anything new the police might uncover."

I watched until his cab turned onto the street, then caught the next one in line, asking to be taken directly to the airport.

I arrived back in New York shortly after four and took a cab directly to the tower. When I reached my apartment, I called Lieutenant MacMann.

"I'm just back from Washington," I said. "Could you possibly come over to my apartment?"

"I'll be there as soon as I can. Did you—"

"Yes, I've got most of the answers now."

Chapter Nineteen

As I waited for the lieutenant to arrive, I thought again of Alfred Brodermen and the things he had told me, but I could no longer feel resentment toward him. The cruel hoax was irresponsible, but I remembered his face as he offered to set up a trust for Stelgis and knew that he now felt as repentant as I did about the shabby things I'd done to Margaret Bochmeir, even though I realized that Margaret and Dr. Falstein were exactly right for each other. What pleased me most about Brodermen's attitude was his desire to meet his nephew. How would I deal with Stelgis? With Sophia? Of one thing I was certain: Stelgis must be told the truth. He could survive it; I was sure of it. And I believed that Alfred Brodermen could become a positive force in this life.

Lieutenant MacMann arrived shortly before six. "What was Broderman like?" he asked.

"I like him. He was reluctant to level with me at first, but he finally opened up. I must have your word, Lieutenant, that he won't be bothered about his part in this sad situation. I promised him that—"

"We'll have no reason to bring him into the case, unless he—"

"No 'unless,' Lieutenant. I gave him my word."

"All right. I trust your judgment. Let me have it straight."

I watched his face closely as I gave a detailed account of our conversation.

"Do you think his brother really told Dr. Semminetti about the boy's true father?"

"Yes, I'm quite sure. Peter Brodermen hated him and old Dr. Kara-Kash. After Kara-Kash's death, telling Dr. Semminetti the truth would have been his ultimate revenge."

"And I'd stake my reputation that it cost him his life. Would Semminetti have told the mother?"

"I'm sure he wouldn't. I think the man loves her, in his own twisted way."

"He went to Pan Am's Midtown office this morning and made reservations for two to Rome on the first of August. Do you know what this is all about?"

"He's been asking Sophia to go with him to an appointment he has at a university medical school there. He wants her to put Stelgis in a boys' boarding school in New Hampshire, but she's been resisting, according to Stelgis."

"Well, we can't let him get out of the country. He went to the medical center this afternoon for some ceremony in the chapel."

"It was a memorial service for Dr. Snyder."

"If he had a hand in his death, he would have had to attend. He's a very shrewd man. Here's what I want you to do. I want you to let him know that you're meeting the boy in Central Park next Friday evening, after dark."

"But, Lieutenant, I'm not sure I can do that. He probably won't speak with me now. Perhaps I could ask Stelgis to let Semminetti know I'm going to meet him. He's in and out of the Kara-Kash apartment and—"

"I'll leave that part to you, Doctor. You have a way with people. I never really believed you'd get anything out of Brodermen, but you hit the jackpot. You mustn't be frightened when you go into the park, but keep alert. We'll have you covered every minute you're there. It's the one sure way we have of convicting this man."

"We'll be careful."

"Let me know when Semminetti's been told."

I suddenly felt exhausted after he had gone, physically

and emotionally. When Yong Ha called me from the desk, asking if I'd like to come down and play backgammon, I told him that I was going to bed early.

Sophia called me at nine o'clock, her voice calm and friendly.

"I was wondering, Dr. Golm, if I could ask a favor?"

"You certainly can."

"Would it be imposing too much if I asked you to keep Stelgis tomorrow? I could drop him off at nine in the morning."

"I'd love to have him, Sophia. Perhaps the three of us could have dinner together. I've found a very good restaurant just across the bridge. Please let me make a reservation."

"All right, Gus."

I put the phone down, feeling my hopes rising. It was the second time she had used my first name.

I watched the ten o'clock news, then went to bed, knowing I would sleep well.

I was up at eight the next morning. I ate breakfast and made a mental note that Stelgis and I should go to the supermarket to replenish my empty shelves. I went down to the lobby just before nine, picked up a copy of the *Times*, then went outside to sit on the ramp and wait. The little BMW turned into the driveway exactly at nine. Stelgis jumped out and grabbed my hand, asking if he could go up and see Yong Ha. I nodded and he ran into the building. I started to get into the car to talk to Sophia, then hesitated when I saw the expression on her face.

"I really must run," she said, suddenly smiling. "I can't tell you, Dr. Golm, how deeply I feel about—about the change you've brought about in Stelgis. He's been a different boy. Thank you—for everything." She held out her hand to me. I took it in mine and held it for a moment, squeezing it. She did not flinch or try to pull away. I released it, stepping back, knowing I shouldn't press my luck.

"We'll see you here when you can make it," I said. "Our reservation is open at the restaurant."

She smiled again, then pulled away. I waited, watching, but she didn't look back.

I stopped at Yong Ha's apartment. He was ready to leave for duty and Stelgis was helping him adjust his prosthesis. I hoped he hadn't mentioned our experience in the tunnel.

"I got another exam this morning. I cook dinner. Okay? Jimmy working again tonight."

"Later in the week, Yong," I said. "We're going over to Louie's for dinner, on Nine W."

We went up to the supermarket and bought three large bags of food and carried them back to the apartment. I asked Stelgis if there was anything special he would like to do today. He thought a moment, then said, "Would you like for me to show you through the museum?"

"I'd like it very much but I thought you weren't going there this summer."

"It would be all right if you went with me. I thought we might go to the apartment later. I don't like to leave Sophia alone. She said she'd be gone, but—"

"Where is she going?"

"Oh, she said she was going to buy some new clothes. I think she just wants to get away from the apartment."

"It's pretty bad, then?"

He nodded. "He's after her all the time. Says she's got to go with him to Italy. She's not going. I think she's planning to go away."

"Where?"

"Chicago, I guess, until he's in Italy."

"I've really got too many things to do here today," I said. "We can see the museum on Friday. I'll take the whole day off. Maybe we can take a walk in the park in the evening, like we did the other day. Would you like that?"

"Sure. That big baboon is something, isn't he? Do you know he likes cigars? The keeper gives him two every day. He really does, Gus. And he spits on people when they tease him."

"How do you know that?"

He grinned suddenly.

We went down to the institute, where I dropped off my latest copy with Miss Thomas. Dr. Karsloff was away for the day in Albany, she said, unable to keep satisfaction out of her voice. She promised to hold my copy for his approval before having it typed.

I gave Stelgis a tour of the institute, including the patient-care floors. I hesitated about going to the twelfth floor, then decided that I should. I admitted us with my key and we walked up the corridor. All was quiet and orderly. When we reached the nursing station and looked through the window, Dr. Falstein was sitting at one of the desks writing on charts. Margaret was standing beside him, her hand on his shoulder as she watched. I tapped my key against the counter and they both jumped, guiltily expressions on their faces as Margaret moved away from him. They came to greet us.

"This is my friend Stelgis," I said. "I'm giving him a tour of the place. You two look busy."

Falstein pulled at his beard, a sheepish expression on his face. Margaret looked up at him, some silent communication was exchanged, then she said, "What do you think of this, Gustav?" and held out her left hand. A large diamond sparkled in the ring on her fourth finger.

I met her eyes, smiled and said, "I hope you'll both be very happy. I mean it sincerely. When?"

"In October, when we both get our vacations."

"That's wonderful," I said. "I hope I get an invitation."

"Oh, of course you will." Her buzzer sounded and she hurried out to a room off the solarium.

Dr. Falstein walked with us to the door, obviously embarrassed. "I hope you don't feel any resentment, Golm. I—these things happen and—"

"I know exactly. No explanations needed."

"I'm glad you understand."

He stopped at the door and locked it behind us.

"What's wrong with that guy, Gus?" Stelgis asked.

"I think he's in love. He thinks he stole my girl."

"Did he, Gus?"

"Yes, with a little shove in the right direction."

I took him over to the central hospital unit and up to the twentieth-floor surgical suite and into the amphitheater, where the open-heart team was doing a valve transplant on a young boy.

"Are you up to watching something like this?"

"Oh, yes. I've seen brain, eye and stomach operations, but I haven't seen open-heart surgery."

He watched the team, all seventeen of them, as they moved in harmony, asking intelligent questions, listening carefully to my answers. We stayed almost an hour, then went down to the coffee shop, where we had hamburgers and milk shakes. We were ready to leave when I heard myself paged.

I went to the house phone, dialed "O" and waited, listening to my page call as it was repeated.

"Dr. Golm," I said, when the line opened.

"Where have you been? We've been paging you since one o'clock."

"What's up?"

"A Lieutenant MacMann of the New York police is trying to contact you. Call him at once. Here's the number."

"Get it for me," I said. "I'll forget and I don't have a pencil handy."

I could hear her sigh of exasperation, but the call went through immediately.

"MacMann speaking."

"This is Dr. Golm."

"Where have you been, fellow?"

"Watching open-heart surgery."

"Could you catch a cab and come up to the Thirty-fourth Precinct Station? I'm going to have to take a statement from you. It's over—as far as Dr. Semminetti is concerned."

"What's up, for Christ's sake?"

"When Semminetti didn't leave his apartment yesterday or today, I sent a man up to check. We knew he was in there, but he didn't answer his buzzer. The door was unlocked and our man went in. He found Semminetti on his back, with one of those darts embedded in his chest. He'd been dead only a short time. The apartment was a mess—there had been a struggle. Where is the Kara-Kash kid? I just got back from down there. No one answers in their apartment."

"Can't I come later this evening, Lieutenant?"

"Why can't you come now?"

"I have Stelgis with me. He's been with me since nine this morning."

"Well, there goes that lead! I was certain it had to be the kid. I could come to your apartment again."

"We're having dinner with Sophia. She's going to pick us up here."

"All right. I'll see you in the morning then. I'll have the lab reports by then and—do you think Brodermen could have followed you up to New York yesterday?"

"Anything is possible, Lieutenant."

"What's wrong, Gus?" Stelgis asked as I turned away from the phone.

"Let's go back to the apartment."

"Is Sophia all right?"

"Yes. It's your Uncle Ted. He's dead."

The boy's eyes widened as his hand slipped into mine. We walked out to the street and hurried toward the tower. As we went up in the elevator, he finally spoke. "How did it happen, Gus?"

"They found another of those poison darts in his chest. Do you know where it might have come from?"

"Sure. He had five or six of them hidden in his file cabinet. He caught me looking at them and hid them somewhere else. Oh, Gus—"

"It's all right, Stelgis. Go ahead and cry."

I held him in my arms until he went to sleep. Then I showered and dressed for dinner.

Chapter Twenty

We waited in front of the tower door until six-thirty. I was about to go in and call Sophia when Yong Ha came out to tell me that I had a call.

"You stay with Stelgis," I said, going inside to pick up the desk phone.

"Dr. Golm."

"Hello, Doctor. MacMann. Is the boy with you?"

"Yes."

"I have some sad news for you, and the boy."

"What is it, for God's sake?"

"When we didn't see his mother come back to the apartment, my man asked the doorman about her. He told us she had returned around nine-thirty this morning. The doorman unlocked the door. She's dead, Dr. Golm."

"Oh, my God!" I felt tears coming, tried to speak, but couldn't for a moment.

"Are you all right, Doctor?"

"Give me a moment."

"I understand. She left a note for you."

"Did she—did she kill herself?"

"I'm afraid so. There was a syringe on the bed beside her. It contained strychnine. She wanted to make sure. I've had to remove her body and Semminetti's to the morgue for autopsies. It's mandatory."

"I understand. What can I tell Stelgis? Poor—poor kid."

"Her apartment was a mess too. They must have struggled there first. I've talked to my inspector. She obviously acted in self-defense. Her prints were on the dart. Her clothing was torn. For the kid's sake, he thinks we might withhold some of the evidence, turning the situation around. No one would be harmed. Semminetti killed her, then himself. What do you think?"

"No. This child has been lied to enough. He can accept the truth—he'll know why she did it. I won't lie to him ever."

"I'm glad to hear you say that, Doctor. The note to you was only two lines. Shall I read it to you?"

"Please."

"It reads 'Dear Gus, Please look out for Stelgis. We love you very much. My lawyer will call you.'"

"Can I help with funeral arrangements?"

"Please do. I'm too stunned to think. I felt certain she'd gone home this morning to kill him. It was her only way out."

"I know a sympathetic funeral director over on Amsterdam Avenue. I'll have her body taken there in the morning."

"Thank you."

I went into the lobby men's room and washed my eyes, still in shock. I'd felt the same emotions before after losing a patient, but not as deeply. I gathered myself together, grateful for my years of training and conditioning. I thought of my responsibilities to Stelgis, and knew that I wouldn't get a chance later to call Dr. Karsloff. As I went up to my apartment to find his number, everything that I would have to do began to fall into place. His wife answered the phone, then called him.

"What the hell is it now, Golm? I just got in from Albany, for Christ's sake, and I'm—"

"Sophia is dead, Dr. Karsloff. And so is Dr. Semminetti."

"Oh, my God!"

"The police say he apparently tried to rape her. She killed him, then herself."

"What about the boy?"

"He's with me. She left a note asking me to look out for him. He has no one else."

188

"I'm sorry, Golm. Is there anything I can do?"

"Yes, sir. I've decided not to take the fellowship you offered me. I want to go home for a while. My parents will love to have Stelgis. I can have the directorship of the Community Mental Center there. Maybe I can come back in a couple of years for some experience in child psychiatry. I'm sorry to let you down on the newsletter."

"It's all right, Golm. I may be able to get one of the attendings to volunteer to take it over. Let me know if there is anything I can do."

"I will, and thank you for being so understanding, sir."

Stelgis slept with me that night, sobbing softly, holding my hand. I had told him everything, about his father, his mother and Dr. Semminetti, knowing that shock plays its role in human survival, and how much better it is to get it all out in one great hurt.

There was no funeral service in New York. A few friends came to pay their respects at the funeral home, including Dr. Karsloff and some friends of her father's. We had the body flown to Indianapolis, where it was picked up by ambulance and delivered to Bordentown for funeral services Saturday.

The attorney called me on Friday morning, asking me to come to his office. Stelgis accompanied me. Sophia set up a trust for him and I was named trustee and executor of her estate. The attorney would arrange to have the co-op sold and cancel the lease in Chicago. The furniture would be sold or placed in storage.

Early Thursday morning Stelgis and I drove the BMW down to the hospital, parking on the street by the back garden. I asked Stelgis to stay in the car as I went out to take one last look around.

As I stood in the garden, surrounded by the exotic trees provided by grateful patients, at the flower beds and carefully tended lawn, I felt something about the place that I'd never felt before. Most of the buildings that rose twenty stories above me were named after Hadley and members of his family. Until this moment, Hadley had been only a name to me, always there, like Lincoln and Washington. I thought of the things I'd read about Walter S. Hadley, who had inherited hundreds of millions from his father and grandfather at an early age, with additional millions coming in each year. He had spent his entire life, working harder than most people, just trying to give his money away in a manner that would help his fellow man. This garden had once been a baseball diamond for what later became the New York Yankees. Billy Sunday had pitched his tent here to preach to thousands. Hadley had bought it, then against great opposition, had brought a great university medical school and several of New York's oldest specialty hospitals into a single unit, forming the world's first true medical center, which had become the model for others. The very rich, from all over the world, came to Hadley Pavillion and the Hadley Children's Hospital, the Hadley Eye Institute, the Hadley Neurological Institute—but its primary function was medical education, research and medical care of the city's poor. To have been a student here, or an intern or resident, was a privilege thousands sought each year, but only a few could be accepted. I had been one of the lucky few. The Hadley Fund had provided the loans for my last two years of medical school in Indiana. As I looked at the tall, silent buildings, I remembered my revolving internship through most of them, the patients I'd watched get well, the ones who had died. I knew that I would never feel the same about any place on earth. I would miss it.

I walked slowly back to the street. Dr. Karsloff's white Mercedes turned the corner and came toward me, stopping when he recognized me. I went over to talk to him.

"I was planning to stop by your office and say goodbye," I said. "We're about ready to take off."

"How's the boy, Golm?"

"Feeling better. I loved her, you know."

"Why must you always tell me what I already know, for Christ's sake? I was watching your face the first time you looked at her."

"Thank you for everything, sir," I said, feeling tears forming in my eyes.

"You're beginning to catch on, Golm. We do our best, but some of them die. When that happens, we think of all the things we might have done. At this point, we have only one recourse."

"What's that, sir?"

"We can ask God to instruct our sorrows. Sometimes it helps. I have another damned staff meeting in three minutes." He smiled suddenly, and held out his hand. "Good-bye, Doctor. It's been nice having you with us. Keep in touch."